Praise for His Name Is David

'Beautifully written. Vantoortelboom strikes a powerfully emotive chord'
Irish Examiner

'Stories of people with whom you can really identify'
Provinciale Zeeuwse Courant

'Vantoortelboom's evocative prose plunges the reader immediately into the Flanders of WWI'
Trouw

'A book that leaves a deep impression. From the first page on, it has you in its grip. Containing all the big themes, it is moving, endearing, and beautifully written'
Book of the Month, DWDD BOOKSELLERS PANEL

'Intelligent and well-composed'
De Morgen

'Vantoortelboom writes like a true Thoreau about the almost magical beauty of nature: a nature that also provides him with the parallels that are so important running through this book'
Knack Focus

'A book to get excited about'
NRC Handelsblad

'*His Name Is David* crawls deep under your skin and nestles there'
Humo

'Skillfully constructed—weaving action, introspection and flashback'
De Groene Amsterdammer

'The first pages are immediately of a devastating intensity'
8Weekly

'A discovery. The images that the writer evokes are so strong that you instantly feel connected as a reader. A beautiful story, compelling and moving. Highly recommended'
INGRID HOOGERVORST in *Tros Nieuwsshow*

'Compelling and strongly composed: a beautifully written novel'
Visie

'A novel written in beautiful Flemish about guilt and innocence, responsibility and choice, and the good and evil sides of people'
BOEK

'Every single word rings true. In just a few sentences Vantoortelboom outlines a situation, creates atmosphere, evokes feelings. In an incredibly well-constructed story, he keeps adding stones until a carefully crafted house is born— a beautiful work in book form'
Nederlands Dagblad

JAN VANTOORTELBOOM, originally a teacher, grew up in Elverdinge, a small village in Belgium. He studied English literature in Ghent and at the University of Dublin. In 2011 he debuted with the prizewinning novel *De verzonken jongen* ('The Sunken Boy'). With *His Name Is David*, Vantoortelboom's second novel, he cemented his position in Dutch literature. A bestseller in the Netherlands and Belgium, it was chosen as Book of the Month by the influential Dutch talk show *DWDD*.

VIVIEN D. GLASS is a literary translator from Dutch and German to English. She was born in Switzerland to Irish and Swiss parents and moved to the Netherlands in 1995, where she completed a Bachelor's degree at the ITV University of Applied Sciences for Translation and Interpreting. She currently lives and works in the beautiful medieval city of Amersfoort, and enjoys attending translation and poetry workshops whenever her schedule allows. Her published translations include works of fiction, non-fiction, poetry, children's verse, and more.

His Name Is David

JAN VANTOORTELBOOM

His Name Is David

Translated from the Dutch
by Vivien D. Glass

WORLD EDITIONS
New York, London, Amsterdam

Published in the USA in 2019 by World Editions LLC, New York
Published in the UK in 2016 by World Editions Ltd., London

World Editions
New York/London/Amsterdam

Printed at Lake Book, Illinois, USA

Library of Congress Cataloging in Publication Data is available

ISBN 978-1-64286-012-2

First published as *Meester Mitraillette* in the Netherlands in 2014 by
Atlas Contact

This project has been funded with support from the European Commission. This publication reflects the views only of the author, and the Commission cannot be held responsible for any use which may be made of the information contained herein.

 Co-funded by the
Creative Europe Program
of the European Union

The translation of this book is funded by the Flemish Literature Fund
(Vlaams Fonds voor de Letteren - www.flemishliterature.be)

Vlaams
Fonds
voor de
Letteren

Twitter: @WorldEdBooks
Facebook: WorldEditionsInternationalPublishing
www.worldeditions.org

Book Club Discussion Guide are available on our website.

For my father and mother †

I LEAVE THIS downtrodden life a young man: strong in body, clear in mind. It is not what I want, but I haven't been asked. They've tied me to a post. A few metres behind me is a beech tree, massive on the verge of bloom. Looking through the frost-covered branches, I see blue sky, a trail of cloud slicing across it unhindered. The ground is cold. I feel a sense of timelessness I've never experienced before, as the morning dew slowly seeping into the fabric of my trousers grows tepid. By noon, I'll be as cold as the earth, as the frost on the branches of the beech. As the air.

I lose control of my bladder, staining myself with the comforting warmth of my own body. I shall undoubtedly be forgiven the disgrace.

Spring is near. The days are lengthening already. Soon, the sun will mercilessly smother winter. Then man and beast will bow down expectantly, and new life bloom: butterflies emerging from cocoons, buds bursting into blossom. They will mate fluttering over my soldier's grave, the butterflies.

The men in front of me are tossing crumbs to the squabbling magpies and jackdaws. In the field lies the carcass of a cow, one of its legs pointing stiffly at the sun. Then I see him. Galloping straight toward me, he jerks at the reins just metres away from the men. The stallion rears up, forelegs flailing in the air, spraying flecks of froth around.

Clods of earth fly from its hooves. A soldier rushes up, grabs the reins and calms the horse with loving strokes over its muzzle. The officer dismounts, nods at his freezing men and turns to look at me. He is my executioner. I hope he's a good man. A righteous human being. Not a monument to a murderous war. Looking up at him hurts my neck.

'Is there anything you want to say, David? A last confession, perhaps? I can arrange it for you,' he says.

He's nice. He knows my name. Two frost-blue eyes in a weary face. I could say that I don't believe in life after death, that I've never yearned for a god who is dead and buried, that my father taught me faith is a weakness of mankind, and that a confession, to me, would make as little sense as it would bring me salvation. I could also say that, though I honestly tried to make something of life, my mother's forgiveness is the only thing I want from it now. Looking at him, I know my words would touch him. His hair looks like a wilted dandelion. He would make an effort to listen to me, to understand, and perhaps make a few meaningful remarks. Will his face be the last thing I see as the bullets cut through the tissue of my heart? I don't know his name.

Or should I close my eyes when the rifles are shouldered and the black barrels aimed at me? Look to the inside? At my little brother, crawling through the garden on his knees; at my parents, standing in the small, sunlit kitchen together? Or at the class I used to teach, the boys of Year Six? Marcus in front. They would undoubtedly come to my rescue. Brandishing their wooden sabres and bows. Their hands, which must have grown even larger and coarser by now, unfastening the ropes around my wrists, cutting the strands with the pocket knives they aren't allowed to carry.

I'd better not think about the two loves of my life.

A command rings out. The soldiers take up position

behind a line. Standing closer now. I look at each of them in turn. They are strangers. I turn my face to the side, pitying the soldiers of my platoon who are forced to watch from a distance, and shake my head at the officer, who is still bent over to talk to me, asking if there is anything he can do. Then he suddenly falls silent. He has understood. He realises that at this stage, words would be nothing but a hindrance.

Am I afraid? They're about to kill me, after all. Aiming at the white ribbon pinned to my uniform, on the spot behind which my heart is hammering away. So loud, I hear it thudding in my throat, in my temples. The heartbeat of the life they want to take from me.

I'm not afraid. I did my best.

WHEN THE TIME is ripe, the fledgling chicks clamber to the edge of their nest and jump. Occasionally, one ends up floundering in a puddle, others are plucked out of the air by a bird of prey before having felt the power of their wings. The majority, however, flap away into the distance, their tiny bird hearts driven by a primeval power. Just like I did, on the day I closed my parents' front door behind me and soared to Ghent railway station like a young seagull, taming the turbulent wind beneath my feathers. Despite the suitcase I lugged with me, my feet hardly seemed to touch the ground as I walked to the station, heart pounding in my chest. I had taken my leap and no one around me had the faintest idea: the man in the three-piece suit crossing my path with his walking stick stared straight ahead, the costermonger didn't even notice me walk by. Not even the railway official who pushed my train tickets over the counter toward me with stubby fingers knew I was flying the coop that day, to a corner of the country I'd never been before; though he might have recognized the hope in my eyes, the restlessness in my limbs.

I pulled myself up by the metal pole, gripping my suitcase tightly, and looked for a window seat. My destination was Ypres. From there, I would take the tram to Elverdinge. It was early in the morning; I expected to arrive shortly after noon. I'd never heard of the village of Elverdinge until that particular morning about a week ago, when Father uttered the name at the table. I did know a little about Ypres, the city of cats. In the Middle Ages, cats were thrown from the roof of the Cloth Hall for good luck.

The smoke of a cigar curled upward. I watched the plume of smoke as it dragged itself over the back of the seat like a ghost, drifting toward me. That morning, my father explained to me that the name of Elverdinge was a male first name, derived from the names Athal and Fritho by a list of phonetic laws (which he also recited to me). He had read up on it, had even discussed it with a professor. I was drowsy and hungry. Besides, I'd become used to his reeling off long lists of the most trivial facts. Ever since my little brother's untimely death, almost four years ago at the time, he had dedicated himself with even more tenacity than before to Professor Pekhart's theory of the Quaternity. Knowledge, in the useless form of randomly amassed facts, had become his faith, had lifted his spirits again after a deep depression. Never needed a confessional, a holy water font or the Blessed Trinity, he said. Mother was frying eggs and a juicy slice of bacon. The smell drove the night air out of the kitchen. My father went on talking. I sat out his speech, and after a long pause that seemed to signal its end, tucked into the breakfast placed in front of me.

Afterward, he asked me how much I remembered of what he'd told me. Wiping my mouth on the dishcloth, I mumbled something about founding father Elverd and his followers. He was silent for a while, before reiterating the whole string of phonetic laws that had led to the place name Elverdinge, and closing with the remark that science and knowledge were based on repetition. It was one of the things Professor Pekhart had taught him. Then he rose, bent down to me and shook my hand across the table, congratulating me on my first job as a teacher in Elverdinge. I sat rooted to my chair. Had he gone mad overnight? Elverdinge? Mother wept, rubbing her expressionless eyes. She sat down beside me, on what used to be my brother Henri's chair, and started buttering a slice of bread with shaking hands. I didn't dare look at her for very long, out of fear of what I would read in her eyes. These days, my parents rarely sat on the sofa together the way they used to, a cup of coffee with a drop of milk on the table at their feet. When my father wasn't working, he spent his time in the shed. I was in the way. I was the wedge driven deep into the log of their marriage. After Ratface's death—how he used to laugh about the nickname I had given him—I went to university, even though I no longer wanted to. They made me. I did my best. The academic years flew by almost in a haze, as if time itself wanted to get away as quickly as possible from the day Ratface died.

'I have been able to get the position for you,' Father said. 'It took some doing, but you are to be the teacher of Year Six at Elverdinge boys' school.' Mother stared at the slice of bread that was still lying on the board in front of her, open and glistening with butter.

'Thank you,' I murmured.

'It is time,' Father said.

He was putting on a brave face.

'Time you stood on your own two feet.'

I nodded, surprised at the feeling of excitement and adventure bubbling up in me.

They gave me an envelope with money. To buy food and coals in the winter—expensive things, Father said. And a suit, as a schoolmaster should always look his best, Mother said. She had folded the slice into a sandwich.

'You are expected at the school next week. So you can get to know the place. The pupils won't be there of course, it's still the summer holidays. But you'll meet the Mother Superior, and get to see the timetable, books and so on. You can move into the house I rented for you. Everything has been arranged,' Father said.

I thanked him. They were holding hands. I had not seen them this close together for a long time. My father's side whiskers looked like tufts of wool torn from a sheep. I tried to swallow the lump in my throat.

The closer we got to the village of Elverdinge—the tram had just passed the stop in Brielen, the village before Elverdinge—the edgier I felt. Wheat country. Meadows with islets of daisies and buttercups. Fields of maize. Everything slowly drifted past me. Occasionally, some boys would leap on the footboard to chug along for a bit before being chased off by the ticket collector. My belly rumbled with a mixture of excitement and fear. It was one of those summer days on which the sky was blue from morning till night. A cheerfully bright pale blue at first. And later, after sunset, a deep and melancholy indigo. I could make out the grey outline of a hill on the horizon. I had never been this far to the west of the country. The tram passed the first houses, and I could hear the driver's call over the click-clacking of the rails and the whistling steam. The ticket collector sprang to his feet, shouted 'Elverdinge station' and disappeared into the next carriage, shouting the same thing again.

We came to a halt opposite the Belle Vue pub. A red flag flapped above the door. Without a glance at their passengers, the stoker, engine driver and ticket collector hurried inside. I put my hand on my suitcase, which I had placed in the aisle beside my seat. Only after the last passenger had walked past—a woman carrying bags that were bursting at the seams—did I leave the carriage. I walked toward the church tower and stopped in front of a large town house.

Two square herb gardens bordered by boxwood hedges flanked the path to the front door, accentuating the building's symmetry. The door swung open, and seeing a man in a black cassock and a wooden cross on a string around his neck stroll out, I realized it was the presbytery. I wanted to go on, but the priest motioned me to wait. He hastened toward me, leaving the door ajar.

'Mr Verbocht?'

My surprise must have been written all over my face, as he went on to explain to me in detail how he had reached that conclusion. He also knew about my appointments both at the boys' school and with Mr Vantomme, the landlord of the house I would live in during the coming school year. To my annoyance, he'd even made inquiries about my appearance.

'So you see, I recognized you the moment I saw you walk past,' he said. 'I would like offer you a cup of coffee, but I'm about to conduct a funeral and need to make some preparations.' He said it with the same seriousness he had put into his earlier explanation. 'I'll pay a visit when you are properly settled in.'

'All right, Father,' I said.

He shook my hand and went back inside. I heard the bolt slide across. I hadn't gone ten metres when I heard footsteps and he was standing behind me again.

'I forgot to tell you, the boys' school and your house are that way,' he said, pointing his arm to the other side of the crossing where I had got off the tram.

'You've been given the addresses, I hope?' he asked.

'Yes, I have. Thank you, Father,' I said. I made no move to follow his instructions. He gave me a doubtful look, twiddled his thumbs for a while and eventually turned to go, glancing over his shoulder one last time before disappearing between the two angular herb gardens. I decided to continue my walk. I had not been given an exact time I should be at the school. One thing he didn't know, at least. Further on, I came to a surprisingly plain square paved with rounded cobbles. From the corner of my eye, I saw the door of the pub on the corner opening. An old man was placed firmly on a stool in the fresh air. Bending over, he spewed a thick stream of vomit on the ground between his shoes. The man who had pressed him down on the chair, and who now seemed to be watching over him, was short but broad-shouldered. He noticed me. I said hello. The bell of the bakery door tinkled and two boys came out, digging their fingers into the white, round sides of the loaves they carried. They shot me a guilty look, stuck out their tongues and ran away. I turned round and started walking in the direction of the boys' school.

THE MOTHER SUPERIOR placed the list of names on her desk. Each name was marked with a stern black dot. She read them out loud, rhythmically tapping her index finger. I listened, more to the way she read than her actual words. When she stopped and looked at me, I was afraid she would ask me to repeat the names. For some reason, one name *had* registered: Marcus Verschoppen. I don't remember what made it stand out from the others, as she went on to tell me some trivialities about each of the eight boys' backgrounds. She hoped I would remember the facts, though her tone of voice, punctuated by her ticking nail, did not seem to express much confidence. She nevertheless considered it her duty to provide a new teacher with all the relevant information. Could it have been her slight hesitation when reading the name, as if silently saying more than she put into words, making the rhythm of her ticking finger falter? She ended by saying I was in luck, I'd be able to see the boys, if I wanted to, because at this very moment they were being taught—she hastily thumbed through a little red book lying on the desk before continuing—Catechism in classroom four. Experience had shown that the boys found learning the texts by heart difficult, so they started them early, in August. I suddenly wondered how on earth my father had managed to get me a job as a teacher in a Catholic school. I wasn't christened, hadn't attended church as a child, had not received my first Communion and had never been instructed in religious subjects. The finger had stopped tapping and was frozen in mid-air like a hook.

'The classroom is at the end of the corridor,' she said. The hook straightened out as she pointed in its direction. 'Incidentally, it will also be your classroom.'

So there I was, on a Friday afternoon under a sunny cotton-wool sky, peeking in through the window of my classroom. And there they were. Caught in a shaft of light slanting down from the tall window. My class. The boy in the first row was sitting on his own. He was wearing a smart white shirt. His hair was combed to the side, parted on the right. I would have bet my last cent on his name being Marcus Verschoppen. I recognized the twins, too: scrawny, ginger-haired boys. I looked at the sombre walls, the portraits of the Belgian Kings, the cupboard with its halo of grime, and high above the blackboard, directly over the portrait of King Leopold ii, Jesus Christ.

In my mind, I started decorating the almost maliciously bare classroom with wall charts, drawings by the boys and poems. I imagined the children's voices and the music that would bring it back to life. I would even put these abandoned windowsills to use. I jumped when a hard object hit the window with a bang, cracking the pane. It was then they spotted me—a new face, caught peering in through the window. They stared at me for several seconds, united in uncertainty, until the lips of the boy in the second row moved. Then came the laughter, collective, a bomb of voices exploding into the outdoors through the gap underneath the door. I turned and walked away.

'**DAVID?**'

'David?'

Opening my eyes, I saw my little brother's head as a dark patch in the semi-darkness of the room. He was sitting upright, his knees pulled up. A block of moonlight tumbled in through the skylight, from nowhere.

'What is it?'

'Why don't bears have long tails?' he asked.

I sighed. 'I'll tell you in the morning.'

'No! Now!'

He used to do that to my parents, too. Every time they went to bed, he would be sitting cross-legged in his cot, wide awake. My mother said it was the fault of the noisy steps, that the creaking woke him. He didn't make a sound, until my parents had changed into their nightclothes and climbed into bed, and the house had gone eerily quiet— then he started. Question after question. I was sometimes jolted from my sleep too, in my room on the other side of the landing. Not by his reedy voice, or Mother's answers. But by Father. By the sound of his spanking my brother's bottom to get him to stop. Or his thundering string of curses just before the spanks. Then came the crying, which only stopped when Mother got out of bed and cradled him in her arms. They argued about it. Mother wanted to keep my brother in their room a little longer, while Father, who had to get up at the crack of dawn to go to work, wanted to throw him out, cot and all.

His questions were usually about animals. That was my doing. During the day, I dragged him through the garden where we lifted the patio flagstones and watched the earthworms, ants and woodlice panic as the roof of their world disappeared. Some frantically tried to crawl away, others scrambled through exposed tunnels, creeping and writhing over each other. We bored into holes and crevices with sticks, digging out eggs and larvae. Then we would stroll down the gravel path to the kitchen garden without giving the garden shed, its windows covered in fairy-tale cobwebs, a second glance. To the hedge. That was the boundary. Pointing through the hornbeam hedge to the woods, I told him that large, wild animals lived there: foxes, deer, badgers. Even wild boars with curved tusks. Bears and wolves, too, I whispered with wide-open eyes. At that point, he'd turn round and run inside. In the evening, the questions rose like bubbles in the descending silence of the night.

'Mum? Mum?'

'Shush. Keep it down. Dad needs his sleep,' Mother whispered.

'How many wolves live in the woods?'

'Wolves? Silly boy. There aren't any wolves here.'

'But David says there are.'

I always giggled when I heard that.

'David is pulling your leg,' Mother said. 'I'll box his ears tomorrow.'

She never did.

'And bears?'

'No bears, either.'

'Mum?'

'Go to sleep now, or Dad will get angry.'

The morning I woke up to the sound of axe blows and cracking wood, I knew at once what was going on. Looking out of my dormer window, I could see Father chopping up the cot. The image shocked me—the violent blows of the axe, the same one he used to chop the chickens' heads off.

'Four's the perfect number,' my father told me when I had run downstairs to join him. 'There won't be any more.'

He was dragging the chopping block into the garden, to hack the planks into even smaller pieces. His axe came very close to his thumb. At every chop, I was afraid he would lop off his thumb, black-rimmed nail and all. From then on, my little brother and I shared my bed. I was ten at the time, he was four.

He dug his elbow into my side.

'Why doesn't the bear have a long tail?'

I didn't have the faintest idea, but remembered a story from one of the books Mother used to teach us to read.

'A very long time ago, his tail froze off,' I said.

'No it didn't!'

'Shhh! Be quiet.'

He was silent for a while, watching the door closely.

'So how did it happen?' he asked, once he was satisfied there were no footsteps coming up the stairs and the door stayed shut. Slowly pulling up my knees and clearing my throat with a deep, guttural sound, I tried to remember the rest of the story.

'The monster awakens from hibernation and rises up from the ice valley,' I improvised. Giggling, he tried with all his strength to push down my knees. He had never succeeded before. It gave me time to think, to frame my answer to his question in my mind. The wooden bedframe creaked. He was leaning his full weight against my legs. Slowly, I let them slide down.

'Now tell me!' he whined.

'Well, it happened one very cold winter. So cold, the ice on the ponds was thirty centimetres thick,' I said. I took hold of his hands and held them apart at approximately the right distance.

'This thick?' he asked incredulously.

I nodded, looking at the two round spots in his face where his eyes were. Silver moonlight surrounded his head. I went on.

'Once upon a time, there were a fox and a bear. The bear was very skinny, and the cruel, sly fox, who wanted to play a joke on him, said he would show him a place to find food. The bear knew the fox and his pranks, but was far too hungry to be suspicious. The fox told him to make a hole in the ice, and with his last strength, the bear managed to do it. Then the fox told him to sit on the hole dangling his tail in the water and wait for a fish to bite; he had tried it himself and it had worked like a charm.'

Out loud, the story sounded ridiculous. I knew he didn't believe me, but he hung on my words all the same.

'Then, the hunters came.'

I shouldered an imaginary rifle and closed one eye to take aim, which he couldn't see in the dark.

'And then? And then?'

He pulled down my arm, bending my thumb so far the joint cracked.

'The fox escaped, of course. The bear wanted to, but his tail was frozen in the ice. He was stuck fast. He twisted and turned his bum, while the voices of the approaching hunters came ever closer. Panicking, he pushed and pulled, harder and harder ... until his tail snapped off.'

My brother pondered for a while, then laughed in my face.

'What a load of rubbish,' he said, his voice more breath than sound.

'It is, actually,' I admitted. 'But it could have happened that way. Don't you think?'

'No,' he said. 'It would have hurt the bear, when his tail started freezing. Animals don't like being hurt, either.'

'That's true,' I said, glad he had thought of that himself.

'Sleep tight, Ratface.'

I called my brother Ratface, a name I gave him when he was less than a year old. Not because his hair was short and spiky; on the contrary—it was white and fine, and there was so much of it that people sometimes mistook it for a white cap when Mother took him to the bakery or the butcher's shop in the village. She laughed about it.

'People who say that are talking through their hats,' Father said when she told us.

I called him Ratface because for months, he only had two incisors in his lower gums, and my parents started to worry whether the other teeth would ever come through.

MR VANTOMME LIVED close to the school. I knocked at the door and waited. Then I peeked through the semi-transparent net curtain, but nothing moved. I knocked again. No sign of life. Only by shielding the sides of my face against the sun was I able to detect movement inside, which turned out to be a cat, lazily stretching itself on the back of an armchair. Then I spotted an envelope, folded four times and wedged into a gap in the window frame. I wrenched it free, flattened the paper and saw the name *Mr Bucht – 91* scribbled on it. Inside the envelope was a key. I slipped it into my trouser pocket and walked in the direction of Boezinge, to the house on number 91.

The key didn't fit. I fumbled at the lock, pushed my shoulder against the door while trying to turn the key, tugged at it when that didn't work, forced the key deeper into the keyhole, tried turning again, but the door wouldn't open. Maybe I could get in through the back door. The garden was a mass of weeds. The key didn't fit there, either. At the back of the garden, I saw a wooden shack with a heart carved into the door. I went back to the front and decided to kill the time sitting on the doorstep. Involuntarily, my thoughts wandered. The boys I saw earlier that day. Rat-face could have been one of them. I had become used to the moments my thoughts turned to him, to seeing flashes of his presence in everyday objects, in animals, in the movement of an arm or a leg. My bum was starting to hurt. I stood up to walk back to Mr Vantomme's house. This time, he was at home. I introduced myself politely and shook his hand. He smacked his lips. When I told him the key didn't fit, he gave me a bewildered look, turned on the heels of his threadbare slippers and mumbled something to a row of photographs as he shuffled past them down the hall. He could hardly walk. I thought I saw some kind of lump between his legs, but decided that had probably been a pocket of air caught in the fabric of his oversized trousers. A moment later, a similar key was stuffed into my hand. He assured me this was the right one and apologized for the misunderstanding, saying he was but an old man, burdened with a failing memory. He asked me whether I had brought my wife and children along, as life would be lonely without them. And did I want a cup of coffee, because his wife had been dead these ten years and now his bitch Penny had also died last week.

'Cancer,' he said pityingly. 'Body covered in lumps. Same as my own late wife. Can such a disease be passed from humans to dogs? Through a flea or mosquito bite, perhaps?'

I said it didn't seem likely to me, that it was kind of him to offer me a cup of coffee, but that my journey had tired me out and I would prefer to go home.

The lock turned with a click, and the door opened without a squeak or creak. A promising start. The plainness of the living room also appealed to me: a table and two chairs, an armchair in the corner next to the window, and next to the stove, which was a kind of potbelly stove, a larder cabinet.

'Everything a man needs,' I mused. The back door didn't open quite as smoothly. There was the shack with the heart door again. I cleared a path through the thistles and nettles until I reached it. The door handle came loose in my hand and didn't seem to fit the mouldered hole when I tried pushing it back in. Leaving the door ajar, I pulled down my trousers. The seat felt damp, and I realized a moment too late that I didn't have anything to wipe myself with. Some kind of large leaf would do. I emptied my bowels, hoping there was no one around to hear the repulsive noise. Through the cracks in the wall I could see a magnificent pink-orange haze where the sun had set. Standing up reluctantly with wet buttocks, I pulled my underpants up to my knees and hobbled to the weeds, in search of my leaf. Amazingly, I found just the thing, a broad leaf on a thick stem—probably rhubarb. I tore it off, bent over and wiped my backside. A cat in heat was wailing somewhere.

I climbed the stairs to look for my bed. With a bit of luck, it would even be made, though I doubted it when I saw the state of the stairs. Every other step was cracked. A recipe for a broken leg. I wasn't disappointed when I entered the bedroom: there was a bed, even if it looked more like a large trough. And a mattress, too, or rather a bag filled with old straw, but soft enough. No sheets. It would do for now. The nights weren't very cold yet.

I pictured myself lying there. My hands crossed on my belly. My feet side by side. Just like Ratface had lain at his wake. What if I died here in my sleep? Who would be the first to find me? Mr Vantomme? But he had a hard enough time walking, never mind climbing the stairs. He'd send over some handyman or other, in which case my body would be carried downstairs by a complete stranger. Perhaps he'd fall down through the cracks in the steps, corpse and all, giving me a posthumous skull fracture and brain haemorrhage. Blood leaking out of my ears. Soaking my hair. Just like Ratface's. Scolding myself for my cowardly fretting, I turned to one side.

The caterwauling started again, closer this time. After yearning for silence for thirty torturous minutes, I got out of bed and tried to open the attic window. It was sealed shut. Besides, I didn't have anything at hand I could have hurled at the creature, which I suspected was sitting in the roof gutter. Standing outside, in the light of a mottled moon, I couldn't make it out anywhere. I climbed back into my trough, where I tossed and turned before finally going to sleep: the sea was rippling silver. I stared vacantly at the crestless waves. My feet stepped over the glistening silver and onto the sand, which gave way under the heels of my boots. Waves crashing against a distant rocky coast, my footprints walking away from the sea. Everything was silent. And I was alone. No squealing, naked women running up to me, breasts bobbing up and down to the rhythm of their steps. A bank of fog rolled down the beach. Suddenly, a little boy emerged from the fog, walking toward me with outstretched arms. Barefoot. His face a grey patch. Greyer than the fog. Gripped by fear, I walked backward, back into the water, my eyes glued to the grey face. When the seawater was at my lips I kept on walking, wanting to drown myself. I woke with a start in the falling dusk, gasping for breath. Several confused seconds later, I heard the cat whining again.

IT WAS ON one of my explorations of Elverdinge's country lanes that I met him. After the heat of the days before, the gentle sunshine was a relief. He was standing at the junction where the straight drive met the winding Hospital Lane. In his right hand he was carrying a bag and a notebook. His left hand was in his trouser pocket. Beside him was an Alsatian, ears pricked. I didn't notice them until I was quite close. They were standing as still as the pollard willows guarding the drive. I looked at him, intrigued by the bag and notebook. It was not a sight I would have expected to see that afternoon, on the last Saturday of the harvest month. I slowed down, saw that the dog had put back its ears and stopped wagging, its tail lying motionless beside it like a black snake. I stopped a couple of metres in front of them.

'Good day, sir,' the boy said.

He took his hand out of his pocket and signalled to the dog, who instantly stopped growling.

'Good afternoon, Marcus,' I said.

He jumped at the sound of his name coming from the mouth of a stranger; he didn't recognize me.

'Does he bite?' I asked.

'Buck won't hurt you.'

I pointed at his bag and notebook.

'Going insect hunting?'

'Butterflies,' he said.

'You will set them free again, I hope?'

'After I've drawn them.'

He tapped on the notebook with his index finger.

'May I see your drawings? Only if you don't mind,' I added quickly when I saw his hesitation. But he carefully placed his bag on the ground and handed me the sketchbook. His fingers looked stubby, the fingertips plump. They didn't match his lean body.

'Very nice drawings,' I said, impressed by the accuracy of the colours and details.

'Thank you.'

He smiled, scrutinizing me curiously with eyes the colour of hazelnuts. In the distance behind his back, a cart pulled by two draught horses turned into the drive. The man on the box shouted something and a whip smacked down on the horses' backs. Marcus had heard it too, and turned round. We stood to one side in the grass. I was still holding his sketchbook as we waited for the approaching cart, which left a cloud of dust and sand in its wake.

'I have to go,' the boy said in a worried tone of voice.

He grabbed the book I held out to him. The cart slowed down but didn't stop. With a jerk of his head, the man ordered Marcus to jump on behind. The dog went first with an effortless bound, but the boy ran after the cart stiffly, trying to place his bag and notebook on the jolting vehicle as it gathered speed before awkwardly scrambling onto it himself. The man didn't look back once. When the whip cracked a second time and Marcus was safely installed in the back, he waved to me.

RATFACE'S ARRIVAL WAS a major event. His scream woke me up, rang in my new life. I had never looked forward to anything so much—at six years old, I had already given up hope of ever having a little brother. Leaping out of bed, I opened the dormer window and savoured the morning air for a moment: a mixture of peppermint, verbena and lavender that rose up from Mother's herb garden. As always, I scanned the primroses and buddleias for sleeping butterflies, wings pressed together, weighed down by dew drops. Then I ran to the door. My fingers already clutched the handle when the realisation dawned on me that I would have to wait for Father. The night before, sitting on the edge of my bed and temporarily adopting my mother's habit of drawing a cross on my forehead with her thumb before I went to sleep, he had forbidden me to leave my room.

'Tonight's the night,' he said. 'Tonight, the baby will come.'

And only once everything was over and my little brother was sleeping in his cot, would he fetch me. I looked at the toys Father and I had made for him together—a pull cart, a rocking horse and a castle—sawn and assembled from the planks he hoarded in the shed. Painted with a home-made mixture of birch leaves, beetroot, coffee and egg, prepared in glass jars by Mother. For the horse's mane, I had searched the fences for wool, which I knew sometimes got caught on sharp protrusions; rubbing against them, the sheep would leave behind tufts of wool like small unravelled clouds. The horse was a white stallion, the mount of knights and princes. I watched the dust in the pillar of sunlight slanting into my room from the window and promised out loud —and for the thousandth time—to look after my brother, to teach him everything I knew, to take him out to play when the sun shone, play games with him at the kitchen table when it rained and protect him from whatever or whoever wanted to hurt him. When my father finally came upstairs, I could tell all was well. His eyes shone. He put out his hand and hugged me. My hand in his, we went downstairs side by side. I bumped my elbow on the banister, but ignored the pang of pain. This was a happy day.

One Saturday toward noon, wanting to help my mother who was preoccupied with my brother, I tried to lift a pot of potatoes from the stove with two thick oven mitts and scalded my arm. I had turned my face away from the hot steam escaping from under the lid and hadn't noticed the pot was tilting. The lid slid off and a slosh of boiling water splashed over my arm. I dropped the pot, my scream cutting through my parents' peaceful Saturday routine. A glass bowl toppled over and smashed to pieces on the floor. Mother wailed, Father quickly carried me outside and dipped my arm into the rainwater barrel, up to my shoulder joint. He was holding me like that when I fainted. I don't know how much time had passed when I came round in the armchair, my mother carefully bandaging my skinned hand that was smeared with a tar-like herbal ointment. There was no supper that evening. When she was finished, my mother washed me, dressed me up and combed my hair, and I walked the long way to the doctor with Father, light-headed and with my pain-free hand in his.

The waiting room was empty, the ceiling high. The chairs creaked at the slightest movement. I counted the heart-beats of the throbbing pain in my hand. At two-hundred-and-fifty-seven, the door opened. I stood up and followed the doctor across a stream of blue tiles to the other side of the corridor. Father closed the door.

'Let's have a look at your arm,' the doctor said to me, removing the bandages. He snorted when he saw the dark-grey ointment and inhaled its stench.

'What is this?' he asked Father.

'A herbal ointment his mother made.' The ointment was so thick and viscous the doctor wasn't able to examine the burn. He turned to a cabinet and took out a tube of cream.

'Apply this daily,' he told Father in a stern voice. 'For a week.'

He turned to face me.

'What's your name?'

'David.'

'Well, David. Come back next week,' he said.

I nodded. He fixed me with his stare until I was so uncomfortable my cheeks started burning with embar-rassment. He had large, brown eyes. Hairs curling at his temples.

Father settled the bill.

THE CHURCH CLOCK chimed six times. It was the first of September. My first day at work. Unfortunately, I was even more exhausted than when I had climbed into bed the night before. I would have had to get a grip, and make myself presentable. Everyone knows a good first impression is half the battle. My skin and hair felt greasy. A ray of sunlight crashed into the room like a silent battering ram, and in the brightness of morning, I suddenly noticed a large, green patch of mould on the wall. Repulsive stuff. Why hadn't I noticed it before? I had time to spare and decided to look for some water and a rag or brush to scrub those armour-plated monsters from the wall. I put my shoes on and walked down the garden path, which was starting to look like a game trail, to the hand pump. To my annoyance, it was out of order, though I could hear a gurgling, sucking sound after pumping for five minutes. I cursed and went inside, aware that I would have to go to the school unwashed and certain that the Sisters—and even the boys—would jeer at my slovenly appearance. It was just as well I used some of the money Father and Mother had given me to buy a new suit. It would go some way to saving the situation. I was too nervous to eat a bite. Unwashed and with a rumbling stomach, but prepared for battle, I went to the boys' school.

I knew they would already be waiting for me. Before going in, I dragged my fingers through my spiky hair, which I suspected the wind had blown into a jumbled mess on my way to school. An insect landed on my forehead, a daddy longlegs. Picking it up gingerly between thumb and index finger so as not to squash it, I threw it up in the air. I thanked whichever power had allowed me to get rid of the creature in time to safeguard my solemn entry. As I opened the door, a thin line of sweat trickled down my temple and lost itself in the jungle of my side whisker.

At that moment, the church bells chimed. I shut the door and stood for a moment, awkward in my suit. Sixteen eyes stared at me: challenging, shy. Marcus smiled. I marvelled at how calm and modest the boy always looked, and how, from the first moment, it had kindled a feeling of solidarity in me. Walking to my desk, I took care not to stumble over the stone step of the raised platform. Their heads turned to follow me. Dropping my schoolbooks on the desk with an impressive thump, I pointed at the cracked window pane.

'We shall talk about this in a minute,' I said. 'First, I'd like to know who you are. Each of you will stand up in turn and tell me four things. One: first name. Two: surname. Three: your father's profession. Four: your average marks of the past year.'

'Whuk?!' exclaimed the wiry beanpole with the shock of hair on the second row.

For a moment, I wavered between going over and boxing his ears for his insolent question and pretending I hadn't heard it. I explained again what I wanted to know, in a sterner voice than before.

'Whuk?!' he said again. I came down from the platform, stood next to his desk, ordered him to stand up. He stood up hesitantly.

'Jef. Schyttecatte. Contractor. And I didn't understand the last thing we had to say.'

Jef was the tallest of the class, and tough-looking.

'Mr Schyttecatte,' I repeated slowly and gravely. 'Truly a fitting name.'

The boys sniggered. Jef eyed me with suspicion. He didn't know what would come next, and whether I was making fun of him. The confrontation with the toughest of the pack—a textbook case. His exercise book lay on his desk. When I lifted my hand to pick it up, he made a movement that thwarted my plans: almost imperceptibly, he planted his feet further apart and tilted his head toward me. It dawned on me he expected a thrashing. Did his reputation depend on it? Up to me, then, to disappoint his expectation, especially since I'd have bet anything he would take the beating without batting an eyelid. He looked at me: strong jawline, lips clamped shut like a boxer's. Besides, I didn't want to hit anyone.

'What does "whuk" actually mean?' I asked.

I had again thrown him off balance. The others, too, looked surprised. After a short pause, he stammered, 'Whuk ... er ... that means that ... er ... I weren't sure 'bout the last thing I were meant to say.'

'Ah. Well, Mr Schyttecatte, you have taught me a West Flemish word. And what is the polite way of asking this of someone who doesn't speak West Flemish and therefore does not know the meaning of "whuk"?'

He pondered the question for a while. I looked around the class and saw a twinkle in Marcus's eyes.

'I do believe Mr Schyttecatte does not know the answer to my question,' I said after a pause, keeping my tone light. 'Does anyone here know how that question ought to be asked? Just raise your fingers.' Marcus raised his finger, but I picked the grimy, stained finger of the boy two desks behind him. Not because I didn't want him to succeed, I wanted another boy to say it to make sure Marcus wouldn't become the target of Jef's resentment.

'What did you say!'

'Correct!' I said. 'And what is the name of the boy who has given this crystal clear answer?'

'Roger!' he said, as proud as punch. I noticed Jef looked more relaxed, and slightly bewildered, as he realized he wasn't going to get the thrashing that would have strengthened his position as leader of the pack.

'Again! And correct this time, Mr Schyttecatte!'

More sniggering. I made sure to keep a friendly voice, but a stern look on my face. He wanted to sit down again. I had to end this performance before it could backfire.

'Jef. Schyttecatte. Contractor. Fifty-seven per cent.'

'Good! Sit down!'

I nodded at Roger.

'Roger! Malfait! Farmer! Eighty-three per cent!'

'Walter. Soete. Postman. Fifty-four per cent.'

The twins desperately searched their memories but could not retrieve their marks. They exchanged embarrassed looks and lowered their eyes when it was their turn.

'Marcus. Verschoppen. Farmer. Ninety-five per cent.'

I finished by telling them my name. Now that the first lesson was about to begin in earnest, I decided to forget about the broken window.

'THE FOUR OF us together like this is just right,' Father said after dinner one day, tilting his chair on its back legs, his belt loosened. Mother was picking beans out of Henri's hair and wiped his face with the dish cloth.

'Four is a magical number, you know,' he said to me.

I was chewing on a tough piece of pork, shoving it from left to right with my tongue.

'Do you know why?'

He slowly lifted his left hand to his right and swatted a fly that had landed on it. The squashed insect stuck to the hairs on his arm, a yellowish pulp oozing from its abdomen. With a flick of his hand, he swept the fly under the table.

'Because there are four of us,' I said happily. I had finally managed to swallow the piece of meat.

'Yes, that is true. But if you give the number four a bit more thought, you'll find it is a very special number.'

Mother lifted the kettle from the stove and poured the hot water into the sink. Then she started scouring the pots and pans, tossing her hair over her shoulder from time to time. It was long and loose that evening. She usually wore it tied up in a ponytail. She had a collection of coloured ribbons for that purpose. And a white one for Sundays.

'David,' Father said when he noticed I was daydreaming, 'how many wheels on a cart?'

'Four!' I said.

'How many legs on a table?'

'Four!'

'A chair?'

'Four!'

'A horse?'

'Four!'

'Why?' he asked.

'Because the cart, the table, the chair and the dog would fall over otherwise,' I said.

'The horse,' Father said.

'Yes, the horse!'

'That's correct,' he said, pleased I had followed his train of thought. 'Four creates stability, it allows things to stand firm.'

'We don't have four legs,' I said.

Mother glanced at me over her shoulder.

'True. And we are nowhere near as steady on our feet as all the other mammals. Push someone unexpectedly and he will fall. You can't push over a horse or a cow, even if they don't expect it,' Father said. 'Besides, we do have four limbs.'

I agreed with him, but added that I would be able to push over a mouse.

'Other things come in fours, too,' he went on.

'Have you been chatting with some professor again?' Mother asked. He ignored her question, eager to finish his lecture on the number four. But the word 'professor' was used regularly at mealtimes.

'There are four seasons, four points of the compass, four elements and four temperaments.'

I wanted to ask what elements and temperaments were, but had the feeling he was now talking to Mother, as he was watching her backside as he spoke. The Friday ribbon was red. This ribbon was different from the others: it was perforated and had scalloped edges, like the leaves of our oak tree. Ratface, who had been strapped to his chair all this time, was getting bored. He tried to clamber out. Mother asked Father to unfasten Henri and put him down on the floor.

'David, do you know what else makes four so special?'

'No, Dad.'

'It's the only number whose meaning is identical to the number of letters in its name. F-o-u-r. Four letters.' He laughed.

I understood, and looked up at my father in awe.

'The entire visible world is based on the number four,' he philosophized. I picked at a dried-up piece of food on the table top.

'And even more than that—there's a fourth dimension, namely time.'

'That's enough now,' Mother said. 'It's too much for the boy to take in. And for us,' she added, laughing.

'May I leave the table?' I asked.

'Yes,' she answered.

Ratface started to scream and batter his chair with his fists. Finally, Father stood up, unfastened him and put him down on his hands and knees. He immediately crawled after me. Father took the dish cloth from the shelf, joined Mother at the sink and starting drying the pots and pans.

MARCUS VERSCHOPPEN. A boy with thick black hair and a perfectly cut fringe. He walked with short steps, as if afraid of breaking. The other boys regularly followed him around, marching over the playground as stiff as boards, only to start shoving each other when one of them bumped into the other or threw up his leg just a little too high. Marcus knew they did it. During playtime, he stood with his back against the wall, hands beside his hips, palms pressed against the bricks. Always in the same spot, where his nails had scraped a slight hollow into the granular surface of the bricks. From there, he watched as the others resumed their game, watched their flexible bodies and double-jointed knees and elbows as they jostled to steal the ball from each other. There was no envy in his gaze, rather admiration. Sometimes he straightened up, lifting the top of his head half a brick higher than before. Toward the end of the break period he would finally summon up the courage to leave the wall and stand on the edge of the playing field, just close enough not to get in the boys' way, and out of reach of their flailing arms. On such moments, I could tell he was bursting to join in, to fight for the ball and perhaps even deliver the occasional kick or shove himself. He never allowed himself to disrupt their game, however.

Marcus's eyes never hid the fact he knew the answer before I had finished the question. He would bend over, pick up his pen from its groove and scribble the answer into his exercise book. When four o'clock had passed and the classroom was empty and silent again, I would rummage in the belly of his desk to fish out his exercise book and find that he had jotted down all the correct answers. Without smudges or scratches. And in perfect handwriting.

One day in the first week of school, I noticed that he lingered after I had dismissed the class. He was placing his books in his satchel with deliberate slowness while the others were already outside, their chattering voices dying away in the distance. I was sitting at my desk writing the chores for the next day in my diary. He fastened the straps of his satchel, and after a moment's hesitation, mustered all his courage and walked up to me.

'I'm sorry I didn't recognize you last Saturday,' he said.

'That's all right, Marcus,' I said, surprised that a boy his age would apologize for such a thing.

'I never usually forget a face,' he said.

'A very useful skill for an artist.'

He nodded.

'After seeing you on my walk that Saturday, I wondered how you manage to draw the butterflies. Surely they would have to hold very still for you to get a proper look. How do you do it?' I asked.

The worried expression vanished from his face as he started talking. 'I've got a small bottle of ether in my bag. I put a drop on a piece of cloth that I spread out on the bottom, and when I've caught a butterfly in it, I close the bag—just for a moment, mind, too long is bad for them. Just long enough, so the butterfly is drugged.'

I nodded with interest.

'Then I spread its wings. I never pin them down,' he hastened to add, 'I just let them lie there. And if they come round too soon, that's too bad. They are free to fly away again. I must have drawn a hundred half-finished butter-flies.'

'That's clever,' I said, impressed. 'Most boys your age are more interested in pulling out the butterflies' wings, or burying them alive.'

He looked at me in horror.

'I mean ... of course I'm not saying you should do that, or that I ever did it as a boy, I didn't; but I knew plenty of boys who did ... '

I was lying. I didn't really have any playmates as a boy, and Ratface would never have done such a thing.

'Well, Marcus. I really think your drawings are very beautiful. I would like to see all of them one day.'

'Thank you,' he said.

'Perhaps you could bring them to school with you.' He dropped his gaze to the floor.

'I meant for me, Marcus. Not to show the other boys.'

'I'll do that, sir.'

'Go on home now,' I said. 'Or your parents will worry.' He picked up his satchel and left the classroom in high spirits.

On my way home, I made a mental list of a number of ne-cessities I believed every tenant should have at his dis-posal: a blanket, a comb, soap, a wash basin and perhaps, if available, a decent mattress. I decided to call on Mr Van-tomme—he was my landlord, after all, and should have provided me with at least some of these things. He was sitting on a chair in the doorway, smoking a cigar. Facing him, I was startled by the bags under his eyes. A black cat was winding a figure of eight around his legs, rubbing its body against his trousers. The enormous lump in his crotch was still there. It looked like a cannonball. He no-ticed my surprise, and told me without batting an eyelid that it was a groin hernia. I didn't know a single piece of proverbial wisdom that applied to this situation—except that it might be wise to see his GP about it, as the hernia was obviously keeping him awake at night.

'Have you come to hand me my cash already?'

'You mean the rent?'

'Naturally.'

'No. There's something else I want to see you about.' But I no longer had his undivided attention. He was greeting a woman on a bicycle, who, in an embarrassed effort to keep the wind from blowing up her skirt, held one hand on the handlebar and the other between her thighs.

'Good day, Godalevakins!'

Flaming past, Godaleva gave him a curt but polite nod. Mr Vantomme watched her until she had turned into Stone Street, turned to me again and asked a second time whether I was about to hand him the cash.

'Actually, I wanted to ask you something.'

'Did you see that posh lady cycle past just now?'

'No.'

'She's the mother of one of your lads. Now what's his name ... the pale, skinny one ... always neatly dressed and in long trousers all summer?'

'Do you mean Marcus Verschoppen?'

'That's him. Well, that was his mother.' He smacked his lips. 'A real beaut', smashing white thighs. The more wind, the better.'

I hadn't had a good look at the woman, though I had caught the nod.

'She's farmer Verschoppen's girl. Beware of him. Jealous as a billy goat. Was in the army as a lad. Even made it to officer. But then he took over his father's farm and ...'

I thought of the green patches of mould on my bedroom wall, the blanket I didn't have and the pump that didn't work, but no longer felt like bringing those things up.

'I think I'll be heading home now,' I interrupted him. 'It's been a busy week, and I need to get everything ready for tomorrow.'

'Fine! Fine! Well, goodbye.'

As I stuck the key into the keyhole, I heard a rustle in the bushes. Curious, I crept toward the sound. I hunched down at the hawthorn hedge, brushed aside a heap of brown leaves and discovered a hedgehog snuffling around. A small specimen. He curled up in a ball when I touched him. The sight of the creature instantly put me in a benevolent mood. I gently picked him up in cupped hands and carried him to my weed garden, where I placed him underneath a couple of boards leaning against the wall. I named him 'Spiney'. It occurred to me I should ask Marcus to draw him for me. Then I walked back to fetch a bucket and poured a dash of water into the hole at the top of the pump. After pumping the rusty rod forty times, I heard a slurping sound and the water started flowing. Rust-coloured at first, then clear. Another step closer to civilisation, I thought with satisfaction as I picked up the bucket, cast a quick glance behind the boards, where Spiney was mercilessly chomping on a worm, and shuffled inside.

That evening, there was a knock at the door. Surprised and slightly annoyed, I answered it. It was the priest. His black cassock blended seamlessly into the surrounding dusk.

'Good evening, Father, do come in,' I said.

'Thank you.'

I offered him my chair and went to fetch the other one from the kitchen.

'I'm not disturbing, I hope?' he asked, glancing at the exercise books on the table.

I shook my head.

He looked around, and after a sniff in which I seemed to detect a certain contempt, he launched into his explanation.

'Actually, my reason for visiting is threefold,' he said. 'Firstly, I wanted to meet a new parishioner, who is, moreover, going to be our new teacher for the children of Year Six. And secondly, I wanted to ask your permission to say a few words about you in this Sunday's service.'

A short pause, in which I just kept nodding mechanically. Why not, I thought. I didn't see anything particularly objectionable in his proposal, given I would not have to be there myself.

'And thirdly, I have a question to put to you.'

'Yes?' I asked, half expecting the question.

'Let's start with reason number one,' he said. 'Would you like to tell me a little about yourself?'

'I would,' I said, though I didn't much feel like it. He must have noticed my sigh. He leaned forward encouragingly. I gave him the short version, saying nothing about the death of my brother. I did talk about Father and Mother. My education. A little about the woods at the back of our house and my love of animals.

When I had ended, he summarized what I had said, but was still fishing for more.

'So you were brought up by your mother?'

'More or less.'

He frowned.

'You said your father worked at the State University of Ghent?'

'That's right,' I said.

His chair creaked. Or was it mine?

'But you were raised a Catholic?'

'More or less,' I lied.

He frowned again. I could tell he had to stop himself from asking more questions on that subject. He managed with an effort; though one more personal question did make it past his lips.

'You don't have any siblings?'

I hesitated.

'I had a younger brother.'

'Ah ... '

'Died a long time ago,' I said.

'That's very sad,' he said.

I said nothing.

'I trust you honour his memory? Flowers on All Souls' Day? An annual mass for him?'

I wasn't really sure—maybe Mother made the arrangements. He looked at me, sensing my doubt. There was a short silence.

'You understand I would like to tell the parishioners something of what you have just told me on Sunday?'

'Be my guest.'

'You will be there, of course?' he asked.

'My parents are visiting that day.'

A blatant lie.

'That's regrettable. Another time, perhaps,' he said.

He stood up, I opened the door for him. We wished each other good evening without shaking hands. Only once I was back on my chair going over the conversation again did I realize he had not asked his question. I wondered whether he had forgotten, but realized it was highly unlikely. He struck me as a man who was always prepared and never forgot things. Perhaps I had already provided the answer.

ON MY TENTH birthday, I was given the most magnificent birthday present ever: permission to cross the border. To slip through a gap in the hornbeam hedge behind the shed and go into the woods. I had badgered my parents about it for years until suddenly, out of the blue, they allowed it. My mother's consent was only half-hearted. She fussed with the ribbon in her hair and looked at me with a worried frown while Father was telling me, handing me a brand new pocket knife to boot. He was enjoying the moment. I leapt up and ran round the kitchen table to hug my parents. My father went on to explain to me how to reach the path into the woods. Starting from the hedge, I was to walk straight ahead for one hundred paces. He had nailed small wooden panels to the trees, which I should follow to the gravel path. At the junction, he had driven a willow post into the ground and painted it white. That way, he said, I would never get lost—the path was a loop, all I had to do was follow it and I would always end up back at the post. Mother had prepared a rucksack with sandwiches and a filled canteen. Overjoyed, and as excited as a puppy about to escape through a hole in the fence, I searched for the breach in the parapet which the hedge had always been for me. I soon spotted it: the moist, white stumps of pruned twigs like the innards of the hedge. That was Father's doing. I crawled through, followed the panels, found the post and set out to explore the woods on my own for the first time in my life. I still remember the way my shoes sank into soft forest soil, the scent of humus, live foliage and mouldered wood I inhaled, punctuated by birdsong.

At lunchtime, I leaned against the trunk of a beech tree to eat my sandwiches. Then I saw him. Out of nowhere, he had appeared just ten metres away from me: an old roebuck, a three-pointer, glorious in his sand-coloured summer coat. I watched, dumbfounded, as he calmly nibbled at the shoots of a bramble bush, white chin in the air. I stopped chewing so as to avoid any movement that might spook the animal. But a wasp landed on a dollop of jam that had fallen from the sandwich on my trousers. I shook my leg. The buck's coat shuddered, chasing away flies. He saw me. The wasp stung. I slapped the insect from my trousers with a sharp swipe of my wrist. When I looked up, the buck had disappeared. Disappointed and with a painfully swollen thigh, I got up and went to the spot where he had been nibbling. There was a fresh pile of droppings, moistly glistening. I saw the tracks his hooves had made in the soil. Then I thought of my brother, and imagined telling him about this magical encounter that night. He would be jealous. I wanted to take him something. Owl pellets were easy to find.

I walked on until I reached an exotic-looking tree whose split bark gaped open like a jacket. Deep purple leaves with thick veins hung limply from its branches. I jumped to the lowest branch, held it down with one hand and carefully plucked off one of the leaves at the stem. The gift he would like most, however, was the skull of a bird—a crow, I reckoned—bleached and with its beak still attached. It was lying at the foot of a silver birch as if on display, there for the taking. I carefully packed it into my lunchbox.

The wood was getting darker, only the treetops glowed in the weakening rays of the sun. The undergrowth rustled here and there, wildlife getting ready for their nocturnal hunt. Reluctantly, I started for home. I'd promised to be back for supper, and was too grateful to my parents to betray their trust.

THE SCENT OF waning summer saturating the air never ceased to enchant me. The sweet aroma of plants and trees, in which life was already going dormant as the flow of sap slowed down. Forest animals, who also sensed the threat of the approaching cold, fleeing to safer places or burrowing deeper into the soil. The fading buzz of a wasp looking for forgotten apples, the screeching geese flying in formation overhead, the daddy longlegs awkwardly sticking to the bricks. It charmed me, reminded me of the past. Elverdinge's Forest Lane especially, with its tall poplars whose foliage was thinning by the day. I took care not to step into the muddy puddles with my only pair of shoes, or get mud on my trousers. The lane belonged to the private estate of an aristocratic family. At this time of the evening, some of the windows of the castle in the distance were already lit. I imagined a library full of bookcases that reached up to the ceiling. And a fireplace with man-sized sandstone pillars on either side. Crackling logs. Perhaps the countess, lounging in an armchair in her nightgown, reading a book while the count, watching her, was lost in a reverie of what else the evening would have in store.

I put my foot in a puddle, cursed. Water seeped into my shoe, soaking my sock. The moon was now in full view: proud and bare, covered in spots, its reflected light floating eerily in the branches of the poplars. At every step, the sodden leather made a wet squelch, and it struck me that robbers in the undergrowth would hear me coming miles away. This is what it must have been like in the old days: hoofbeats on the cobbles, cartwheels creaking over the potholes and bumps. And darkness all around. Then a flash from a barrel. Or a spear in your chest. I hurried to Vlamertinge Street and turned right, until I could see the houses again. Then left, toward the church. I could hear the din coming from the Pumphouse pub from afar. It was Saturday night, and judging by the noise, the pub was packed. I thought I saw someone standing outside—a shadow beside the door, leaning against the brick wall. Probably someone in need of some fresh air, or sobering up. As I slowed my pace, I noticed him politely saying goodbye to some punters leaving the pub. He wasn't tall, but his bearing commanded respect. He saw me approach, followed me with his eyes. Then I recognized him. It was the same man who, at my arrival a fortnight ago, had sat the elderly man on a chair outside the door. I said hello. He nodded at me. I walked on without looking back.

When I arrived home, Spiney wasn't foraging in his favourite spot. There was no sign of him underneath the board, either. After frantically searching every corner of my weed garden, I finally decided to wade through the tall thistles, to places I had never set foot on before. I was convinced he had fallen prey to a fox. Or maybe a farmer, alerted by his dog's continuous barking and whining, had found Spiney rolled up in the grass, ran to fetch a pitchfork and stabbed him to death on the spot. This version of events, which for some reason seemed entirely plausible to me, enraged me so much I punched a hole into the mouldered wood of the loo door with my fist—something I regretted ten seconds later for reasons of decency.

In the living room, I sank down on my chair. I lit a candle

I had bought at the grocer's. A small fly narrowly managed to avoid the flame, then hurtled down onto the tabletop all the same. Leaning over it, I saw one of its wings was singed while the other buzzed in mortal agony. My fingernail put the insect out of its misery.

'DAVID? DAVID?'

'What?'

'Which is stronger, the lion or the tiger?'

'I don't know,' I said. 'They never meet in the wild, because they live in different countries.'

'But what if they did meet?'

'I really don't know.'

'But if you had to choose, which one would win?'

'The tiger, I think.'

'Why?'

'Because it's a bit bigger.'

'David?'

'What now?'

'What's the biggest animal?'

'In the sea or on land?'

'On land.'

'The elephant.'

'Could an elephant beat a tiger?'

'Yes.'

'So the biggest animal always wins?'

'Not always, Ratface—sometimes many small animals can beat one big one.'

'David?'

'That's enough now, I want to go to sleep.'

'Just one more question, David. Just one. Please!'

'All right then.'

'What's the biggest animal in the sea?'

'The blue whale.'

'Would it beat a killer whale?'

'Blue whales are peaceful. Killer whales live in pods. They leave each other alone.'

He sighed, not satisfied with my answer.

'Now go to sleep,' I said.

He lay down, his white hair disappearing into the soft pillow. All I could see of him was the tip of his nose, and the bulge of the blanket where his feet were. At the foot of our bed was a wooden rack. I had built it for him. It had thirty-six compartments. We had pinned nuts and leaves to the backs of most of the compartments, and put the bleached skulls of at least ten different birds and mammals on the little shelves in front of them. There was also a dung-encrusted cow hoof clipping that Ratface refused to let me clean. All the things I'd collected for him during my walks through the woods. Our greatest treasure was the spine, skull and legs of a rat. We had cut out cardboard labels and carefully written the name of each object on them. The rack was almost full. Beside it were jars of owl pellets, lids tightly shut. He was proud of his collection. I heard his breath get slower, deeper. How strange to be lying in a room with bits of animals that had once been alive. I could almost see the birds fly, feel the wind rush through their feathers, the warm sunshine on their backs and wings as they flew high over the treetops or rested on a branch. I wondered what had killed them. A predator? Old age? Then I heard Father and Mother climb the stairs. Mother's hair was going grey, especially on the sides of her head. And the occasional strand in her ponytail. Father's wasn't. Only his side whiskers had a dull white dusting.

'**SIR! SIR! ROGER** pinched me in the balls!'

Walter and Roger had both appeared out of nowhere. It was Monday morning, break time. I had been daydreaming in the doorway, gazing at the low-hanging branches of the old silver birch that was beginning to lean precariously over the wall between the playground and the fallow land next to it.

'Roger! You mustn't do that,' I said placatingly—I wasn't entirely sure whom to believe, though I did know Roger could be a damned little pest.

Roger protested loudly, calling Walter a great big liar, a milksop with no balls. And adding that he should put some more talcum powder on the sweat glands of his feet, because they smelled like dead rats.

'Roger, you're not being very nice today,' I said, struggling to keep a straight face.

'But it's true, dammit. His feet reek worse than the shit in our cesspit.'

'There will be no cursing here,' I said with sudden severity.

Walter nodded. 'It's because I tortured him the day before yesterday, sir. When we held him prisoner down by the mud heaps. The chump's still angry. First we punched his head and then ... '

'Pah. Didn't hurt a bit,' Roger bragged, but I could tell it rankled with him. He also had a slight limp.

'Then what happened?' I asked.

'Nothing too bad,' Roger answered, his face the colour of beetroot. But Walter was only too willing to give me all the details.

'Well, we, the lords of Elverdinge Castle, had beaten the enemy, the Bakelandt Bandits, and taken one of them prisoner.'

'And that was Roger,' I said.

'Yes, yes.'

Walter was dying to tell the whole story, but Roger pulled his arm and said he wanted to play marbles. Marcus was standing on the side as usual, his back against the wall, longingly watching the game.

'We had captured Roger and dragged him to the haunted willow with a rope around his neck. Do you know that tree? It's split open from top to bottom and they say that it's almost two hundred years old. It's just behind the third heap and it's always bare.'

I knew the tree. It did have an almost ghostly appearance if you walked past it in the evening.

Roger smiled wryly, turned round and limped off.

'Well, we tied him to the tree and then ... we ... um ... ' Walter picked at the tip of his nose, suddenly unsure how much to tell this grown-up in front of him, who was, after all, his teacher.

'Well ... Jef'—he pointed an outstretched arm at the playing scapegoat—'pulled down Roger's trousers and tied a rope around this balls.'

'Excuse me?'

I couldn't believe my ears.

'It's true! And he pulled really hard. And Roger *screamed!*'

I was suddenly livid with rage.

'Would you like me to do that to you? Tie a rope around

your small testicles? And give it a good tug?'

I was talking louder than I intended. Startled, Walter recoiled and blanched from his neck to the roots of his hair.

'No, no, no,' he squealed.

'Never do to others what you wouldn't like done to yourself,' I said sternly, trying in vain to contain my anger.

'But Jef ...'

'I'm talking to you, Walter Soete! Don't you forget it!'

My index finger touched his freckled nose. There was a glob of snot dangling from it. Then I sent him away to play nicely with the other boys, who had gathered around to watch like a herd of curious bullocks, Roger, still red-faced, in the middle.

In preparation of their Holy Communion, the boys were given catechism lessons by the nuns on Saturday mornings. I counted myself lucky that I didn't have to give those lessons. Ordinary religious instruction did fall under my duties, however. I had skipped it in the first week because I was too busy with other things and—if I was honest—because I had no qualms postponing it. I knew God wouldn't punish me, confident as I was that he was a fabrication. Even so, I couldn't shirk my responsibility any longer, if only to fire the boys' imagination. I had resolved to take a strictly unbiased approach.

'Sir, sir!'

'Yes, Roger.' The lesson was almost over and I didn't regret it.

'Surely God can't be everywhere at once? Isn't the world too big, and aren't there too many people for that?'

'It seems that there is a part of God deep inside each of us.'

'How so?'

'That is difficult to explain, Roger. Perhaps you should ask Father Storme.'

Roger looked disappointed.

'What I *can* tell you, is that God is more present in some people than in others.'

'But how do those people know? What does it feel like?'

'You're an altar boy, aren't you? Then you should know better than even the teacher,' Jef said.

'Yes,' Etienne said. 'That's true. Except he never sings along 'cos he still doesn't know the songs by heart, and last week he told me he nicked some coins from Father Storme's collection plate, and ... '

'Not true! It's not true!'

I could tell from the shrewd look on his face that it was.

'You're going to hell, you're going to hell!' Jef and Etienne taunted, and the whole class laughed nervously.

'Come now, boys,' I said calmly. 'No one is going to hell.'

'How so?'

'Whuk?'

'Father Storme says that if we eat too many marshmallows and cake during Lent, there's a good chance we will.'

'Or if we don't say a Hail Mary and an Our Father on our bare knees each night before going to sleep, we could go to hell, too.'

'No one goes to hell,' I repeated calmly. 'But if you eat too many marshmallows and cake, you might have to go to the dentist.'

'How can you be so sure?'

That was Marcus. He had been listening silently the whole time.

'Because I honestly don't believe hell exists.' I refused to betray my beliefs, though I regretted my words the moment they left my mouth.

'No hell? So why do our fathers and mothers and Father Storme say there is one?'

'Perhaps you should ask them.'

'And if hell doesn't exist, does heaven?'

Marcus again. The thought crossed my mind that I shouldn't really tell the boys that I personally didn't believe there was a heaven. It would shake their world to its core, and was bound to get me into trouble—perhaps even lose me my job. Inexplicable, that inner urge to say it anyway: 'There is no heaven, either.'

The silence that fell was so complete, the boys seemed almost afraid of each other. I cursed myself, then hastened to answer the next pressing question milling around in at least one head.

'But I do believe in a presence, natural or otherwise, that can be called God,' I said.

Then Roger piped up again. Sometimes I wished I could solder his damned mouth shut.

'And who was Jesus Christ, really? And did he actually exist?'

'The son of God,' Maurice Muylle said.

'And who was his mother?' Jef asked.

'Mary, of course! Numbskull!' Roger said.

'But how can a god have a wife? Doesn't that mean he's a man?'

'Yes! How else could he have had a child?'

'And Jesus Christ was nailed to the cross, wasn't he? But then he arose from the dead. So shouldn't he still be around somewhere?'

'And which of them is the boss? God or Jesus?'

'Or Mary?'

'The father, of course, dimwit! The same as at home!'

'Not in our house!'

I listened to the squabbling boys, at a complete loss for words and unable to give a single sensible answer to their questions. A nasty feeling of hypocrisy, even guilt, had gripped me by the throat with a cold hand, and try as I might, I couldn't shake it off. I wanted to explain everything, my views on the faith, but I had lost heart. I'd said too much already. Marcus was staring at me, his eyes wide. I regretted the few honest answers I had given that day.

MY PARENTS WERE serious people. They didn't talk or laugh much. But our home was not without affection; a safe, warm seriousness, guarded by candle-light when the outside world was dark and wintry. They often sat together, in the armchairs or at the table, drinking coffee with a spot of milk. My mother would read a book and my father study sketches or building plans. My mother was a teacher. She had taught at a primary school for years, but left her job when she met my father and they had me.

As I grew older, I realized my father was a very restless man who needed a quiet environment to check the torrent of thoughts and impressions constantly running through his head. He never showed it, except on that one occasion, when he chopped up Ratface's cot. He worked at the State University of Ghent. He was the man who met the professors' practical needs, doing everything from assembling bookcases for their ever-expanding supply of books and putting up paintings in their offices to maintaining the lighting and heating of the university buildings. One afternoon, he was asked to shorten the legs of a desk and matching chair because a recently appointed professor was very short in stature. Exhausted from rushing to and fro between the different buildings, he politely let slip that it was damned tricky to be in four places at the same time, as was expected of him. As it turned out, the new professor appreciated my father's talents, and a week later, he was promoted to the head of a group of three young trainee handymen.

'A team of four,' he said, winking at us over supper.

We were proud of our father, and the hard work he did. The university had even given him a bicycle so he could get there without delay. He had shown us the bike and done a test run as we watched. We weren't to fiddle with it, or even sit on it.

'A bike only has two wheels,' Ratface said, but no one understood him because he had just stuffed his mouth full of Mother's crunchy biscuit cake.

When Ratface was about seven, we went to the woods together for the first time. My parents made me promise at least a dozen times to look after him. I remember being bewildered and even hurt because they didn't trust me. Something I had read in a book about birds the night before flashed through my mind: condor chicks are mercilessly pushed off the rocks by their parents. Their only hope is to spread their wings and fly. A strange thought at that moment, but I didn't dwell on it; I was too excited about our trip to the woods. So was Ratface, who nodded like mad at everything Mother said and shouted in a shrill voice that he would do everything his elder brother told him.

And he did, that day. He followed me, enjoying himself as only children can. I pointed out the territorial call of the male cuckoo to him, the kee-kee-kee-kee of the sparrowhawk. We found broken eggshells of all colours and descriptions, and tried to guess which bird they belonged to. We watched a pair of squirrels playing in the treetops, until they noticed us and scrambled into the fork of a branch. There was larger game, too—deer, foxes, even wild boars.

Increasingly, he was the one pointing things out to me. He was quicker to notice movements above our heads or in the distance. Then he'd stop, pull my sleeve and point. I didn't usually see anything, the animal having scarpered on our approach. It hurt my pride to realize how much I overlooked.

We built a lair to lie low for a couple of hours, in a spot we knew there'd be game because we had seen tracks and rooted-up soil. We chose a dense thicket, crept under it, cut off twigs with our pocket knives and covered ourselves with them, our bodies blending into the forest floor like a natural mound. But the best was yet to come—suddenly, Ratface touched my arm and pointed. I didn't see anything, but could hear a noise. A few moments later, I saw them too. A female wild boar with her young. Eight or nine of them. I looked at my brother with my finger to my lips. They were rooting in the earth underneath an oak tree, about ten metres away from us. The horizontal stripes of their coats made the piglets look as if they were wearing pyjamas, Ratface remarked afterward, when the boars had left and we excitedly discussed what we had seen. It was a spectacle neither of us ever forgot and which we talked about countless times, under our blankets at night.

'**THE HUMAN HEART** has four chambers,' Father said.

Ratface and I nodded. It was Saturday afternoon. We were sitting around the biscuit barrel on the kitchen table. It was the only day of the week we were allowed to eat as many biscuits as we wanted.

'All insects have four wings,' Father said.

'A cow has four stomachs,' I shouted.

'There are four evangelists,' Mother said. She smiled a little uneasily.

'What's an angelvist?' Ratface asked.

Father glanced at Mother. She snorted, shifted in her chair, picked up the spoon to stir her coffee. Father blew out air through his nostrils. He often did that when he heard something he didn't like, or thought was ridiculous.

'Flies don't! Flies don't!' Ratface squealed suddenly.

Father fell silent, shaking his head at him.

'We have four wisdom teeth,' he continued.

I was still thinking about the flies. I had never noticed that before. Ever since Ratface, the fourth member of our family, had been born, my father had been under the spell of the number four. And his obsession with what he called his 'magic of four' had only deepened over the years. He jotted down everything he could think of about the number in a small notebook, and if he overheard one of the professors talk about it, he memorized what he had said until he was able to write it down at home. I stood up and walked to the window. There was a dead fly on the sill. Blue-green abdomen glinting in the sun. Dark red eyes like blood blisters. I picked up the insect between my thumb and index finger and studied it.

'Ratface is right,' I said.

It took a while for Father to realize what I was talking about. Ratface grinned.

'Then that must be an exception,' Father said. 'There are of course always exceptions.'

IT WAS SATURDAY evening. Time for a walk. I took my jacket from the hat stand and went to the back door, for a quick look in the garden to see if Spiney was back. No sign of him. With a heavy heart, I made my way through a cloud of bloodthirsty mosquitoes, going nowhere. My steps were hastier than usual. Down Boezinge Road, past the junction with Stone Street, crossing Veurne Road. To the church. Beside the church, Bollemeer Lane. A path that always attracted my eyes and feet. But not tonight. I walked on, at a more leisurely pace now, past the large stone water pump on d'Ennetières Square. I paused to watch the play of moonlight and passing clouds in the stained-glass windows of the church. Again, I heard the muffled noise coming from the Pumphouse. Suddenly, the door of the pub flew open and two men were manhandled outside. The man who had shoved them into the street and was now blocking the doorway was called Victor Vanheule. I had overheard the name while waiting at the end of a queue of women in the grocer's shop. Victor. It suited him like a glove. Slamming the door of the pub behind him, he ordered the men to get lost.

But the two unruly figures made no move to leave; instead, they waddled back toward Victor. I watched him brace himself, hands still in his trouser pockets, legs wider apart than before. Without a word, the two men leapt at him, held on to him, puffing and panting—one of them on his knees, his arms strangling Victor's waist, the other trying to punch him full in the face. A well-aimed knee crushed the nose of the kneeling man, whose head and body hit the ground with a crack. Then Victor grabbed the arm of his second attacker with both hands and broke it against the brick door frame by leaning his full weight on it. The sound produced by the breaking bone sent shivers down my spine. Standing in the doorway, Victor looked down at the writhing bodies in the street. A moment later a figure appeared behind his back, took in the scene, immediately ran to a house down the road and furiously pounded on the front door. Probably the doctor's house, I thought.

I had seen and heard enough, and turned to leave. Just before turning round, I caught Victor's eye. I hurried back home, disgusted to the core of my being. Haunted all the way by the crack of breaking bone, the sound of wailing, and Victor's indifferent gaze resting on the broken bodies.

Back home, I went to the back garden in the hope of finding Spiney, so I could wind down in the serene company of a peaceful animal. The rustling, which I could hear even before I reached his board, filled me with joy. When I found him, in the moonlight shadow under the board I had lifted carefully, he was busy biting a huge earthworm to pieces. The worm was still alive, wriggling and writhing, but Spiney chewed on unperturbed. I told myself this was not a case of gratuitous violence; the little creature had to eat, after all. Carefully stroking his spines, I said good night to the rolled-up pincushion he had become.

WALKING THROUGH THE archway to the coal-dealer's, I saw a boy and a man shovelling a cart full of coal in the courtyard. The boy's shovel was so large and heavy he could hardly lift it, let alone tip the heap of coal piled on its blade over the edge of the cart. Sometimes, the shovel tilted sideways and the coals spilled onto the ground. He was coughing. His face was black from coal dust, with pale rings around his eyes. The man was shovelling mechanically, tossing the coal over the edge with ease. It took a while for me to realize the boy was Marcus. Glad to meet him outside the school for once, I went up to him. He started when he saw me, and shot a quick glance at the man on the other side of the cart.

'That'll put some muscle on you, Marcus,' I joked. He didn't laugh, but almost choked coughing. I patted his back carefully, feeling the sharpness of his shoulder blades. Again he looked to the other side of the cart.

'Is that your father?' I asked.

He nodded, wiping spittle from his mouth with his sleeve. It was the first time I saw him wearing work-clothes, a brown leather belt around his waist to keep up the over-sized trousers. The sound of shovelling on the other side stopped abruptly and farmer Verschoppen walked over to us, round the back of the cart. I turned to face him. He said he wouldn't shake my hand, as his was black and soaked in sweat. He was half a head shorter than me, his eyes the deep, piercing blue of a cold winter morning. His face was marked by grooves.

'We must get on with our work, Marcus,' he ordered, said goodbye to me and went back to his side. Sighing, Marcus went back to work. He wanted to demonstrate his strength by shovelling large heaps of coals at once, but half of it had slipped off before the shovel was in mid-air. Bending his back, he swept the fallen coal back onto the blade with his hand.

'Can I help?' I asked.

'No,' he said, scowling at me. At that moment, the coal-dealer came up to me, gave me a hand shovel and told me to fill my scuttle with coals from the small heap. Five centimes a kilo. To be paid inside. He pointed to a stable door on the other side of the courtyard. I thanked him, picked up my coal scuttle and started shovelling.

I soon realized I would have the devil of a job getting the scuttle back home. Now that it was full, I could hardly lift it as I hobbled to the stable door that had been pointed out to me. Behind my back, I heard Marcus coughing again, and hacking up phlegm.

'What's the scuttle weigh when it's empty?' the coal-dealer asked, sitting at a small table with a dog-eared book on his lap and rolling a thick red pencil between his fingers. There was a set of scales at my feet.

'I don't know. I'd guess about six kilograms,' I said uncertainly.

'Guesswork's no good to me. You'll have to tip out the coals so I can weigh the scuttle first.'

Giving me no time to even consider this, he went on.

'Or we can just assume it weighs three kilos, then you won't have to tip it all out and shovel it in again. Take it or leave it,' he said slyly.

I may not have had much cash to spare, but I had all the time in the world.

'I'd rather empty it,' I said.

Grumbling, he pointed to a shelf in a corner of the stable. I poured the coals on it and placed the scuttle on the scales with a thud.

'Seven kilos.'

'You'd have done better accepting my six,' I said with a nervous laugh.

I shovelled the coal into the scuttle again and heaved it on the scales.

'Two francs sixty-five.'

I reached into my pocket, counted out the money.

'Enjoy your walk home,' he said.

I took the coal scuttle, straightened up and walked toward the archway. I heard another coughing fit, and turning round saw Marcus folded over the handle of his shovel. I dropped the scuttle and ran toward him. He saw me coming, shook his head. But I gently pushed him backward and sat him down on a chopping block, then grabbed his shovel. He wouldn't let go of the handle. I looked at him sternly, whispering that there was no shame in accepting help. Everything was quiet on other side of the cart. Marcus let go of the handle and I started shovelling, taking care to match my speed to his father's when he resumed his work. After about an hour, the cart was loaded to the brim. I couldn't feel my arms. Marcus was still sitting in the exact spot I had put him, staring at the ground between his feet. Farmer Verschoppen flung his shovel on the cart and went inside to pay. I looked at Marcus. He had been crying. I put my hand on his shoulder.

'See you on Monday,' I said.

No reaction.

I went back to my coal scuttle. The two men, obviously

old acquaintances, were having a friendly chat. The coal-dealer burst out laughing at something Verschoppen said, and they both looked at me. I picked up my coal scuttle and walked through the archway into the street. I took regular breaks, sitting down on the verge and looking out over the meadows of Elverdinge, at the church tower rising above the treetops, the seagulls circling over the fields. When I saw the cart approach in the distance, I leapt to my feet, picked up the scuttle and walked on. I was hoping Verschoppen would stop and offer me a lift. He gave me an amused nod in passing. Marcus was sitting on top of the coals. He didn't wave.

IT WAS THE last Saturday in November. I went to Mr Vantomme to give him the envelope with the rent I owed. He wasn't sitting in a chair in the doorway now, it had grown too cold for that. He was in the kitchen, in an armchair draped with a fluffy patchwork quilt. I had knocked loudly, and almost immediately, he had called to me to come in.

'Door's not locked,' he called. 'Never is! Not even the half-wits of Elverdinge are stupid enough to steal anything in this dump! No one here has any money! The filthy money-bags all live in Ypres or Poperinge!' He went on ranting as I walked down the hall, glancing obliquely at the portraits of his late wife lining the walls. What an angular face she had. She was wearing a type of headwear I had never seen before, a white linen cap with embroidered edges and ear flaps. The portrait reminded me of a picture I had once seen in the paper, showing the chieftain of a North American Indian tribe in full regalia. Except that her eyes weren't wise and profoundly sad, but small and beady, and glinting with a hardness that must have made the man behind the lens tremble. And then that furrowed face. Mr Vantomme was now shouting that he didn't live in a castle with fifty-metre hallways and where the devil had I got to. Even sitting in the armchair he had to keep his legs wide apart. He was smoking a cigar, the ashtray on the padded armrest of his chair.

'Good day, schoolmaster!'

'Good afternoon, Mr Vantomme.' He spotted the envelope in my hands. Smoke drifted my way. He motioned me to take a seat. I placed the envelope on the table next to me. I had waited for this moment to bring something up that had been bothering me. The envelope was my pawn, though what I wanted from him was of much less value than the amount it contained. He seemed to sense something. I waited. The bulge in his trousers distracted me, its grey bulk staring me in the face. More cigar smoke curled my way, wreathing around my head. It was making me drowsy.

'Do you know about the mould in my house?' I asked.

'Your house?' I didn't rise to that. It was beside the point. A sly diversionary tactic.

'It's spreading uncommonly quickly, and a brush won't shift it. That is to say, it does go away, but comes back immediately.'

'How so? Mould? Never seen no trace of any!'

'But it's there, behind the upstairs cupboard. Come and see if you like.'

'You need to keep the place clean, eh, young man. There mightn't be a woman in your home, but you must lead a cleanly life.'

'I keep everything clean, I can assure you. But the house is damp. There's a constant dankness in the air and the walls are covered in wet patches.'

'How so? Dankness in the air? What are you, a dog sniffing around its kennel with its nose up in the air?'

'Mr Vantomme, as the landlord, you are responsible for your property.'

'Don't talk drivel, man! Want a pint?'

'No. Thank you.'

'A drop of something stronger, perhaps?'

He didn't make a move to lift as much as a finger—it was clear he counted on my turning down his offer.

'Mr Vantomme. You will have to give me a satisfactory answer in this matter.'

I put my hand on the envelope. His face darkened.

He would have to give in if he wanted his money. I sensed my plan was working, though I felt ill at ease. Not that I was afraid. He was just an old codger with a groin hernia, after all. It was the act of intimidation I disliked, and which weighed on my conscience somewhat. But my health was at stake and I was not prepared to make concessions.

'Otherwise, I shall be forced to file a complaint.'

The springs in his armchair squeaked as he shifted forward with difficulty, waving me closer as if he wanted to whisper a secret in my ear that not even the lingering spirit of his wife could be trusted with.

'Mr Verbocht, listen here.'

I leaned toward him.

'You don't want to get off on the wrong foot, eh? You're new to Elverdinge. You need to make friends, not enemies. I hear things about you and they aren't all good. Don't look so surprised. You don't believe me? You've already stepped on the toes of a number of people here. And those fellows don't just forgive and forget. No, schoolmaster. Men like them are quick to take offence, and settle their scores in their own time.'

He nodded emphatically as he sank deeper into his armchair to take the weight off his balls. I couldn't imagine whom I might have offended, except perhaps the priest, since I hadn't been to Sunday Mass a single time.

'This has nothing to do with the matter of the mould, Mr Vantomme,' I said feebly.

'Tut tut. It has everything to do with it, dear schoolmaster.'

He picked up the stub of his cigar that lay extinguished in the ashtray, lit a match, drew on the stub and again blew the smoke at me. The balance of power seemed suddenly to have tipped in his favour. His last, enigmatic remark had hit home, draining my resolve and confidence. He observed me silently, head tilted, cigar stuck to his lips.

'Mr Vantomme. I find it regrettable that, though I have asked you courteously, you don't seem to be prepared to honour my request of sending someone over to eliminate the mould once and for all. As a tenant, I have rights, and you as a landlord have obligations,' I added with schoolmasterly emphasis.

'Listen.'

He leaned forward again.

'I shall now meet you halfway and tell you something everyone here already knows. Not for the sake of your blue eyes, believe me—I think you're a sterling lad. Farmer Verschoppen owns that hovel. Not me. So don't forget to mention that you're pressing charges against *him*, down in Ypres.'

'But ... '

'Quite.' He held out his hand to receive the envelope. At that moment, I felt the sting of a fly. The little pest was sitting on the back of my hand. I picked up the envelope with my left hand and squashed the insect with it, mercilessly, astonished that this scaled-down version of a bluebottle would have a sting. Then I handed the fly-smeared envelope to Mr Vantomme.

ONE EVENING, A man walked into our kitchen. Mother was frying sausages with onions. I was draining the potatoes. Ratface was noisily setting the table. All of a sudden, the door swung open and the man stood among us. It was Father. But then again, it wasn't. He kissed us good evening and immediately went to the cupboard to fetch his notebook. He didn't take off his jacket. All three of us stopped what we were doing and stared at his back. Something was going on. None of us was sure what. He looked the same. But his gait, his look, even the way he sat was different. More vigorous. He had the deep calm of a rock. Even more than when he stepped back to examine his work after putting the finishing touches on a bookshelf or cupboard. That evening, his notes, which usually amounted to a few words or even just a single letter and rarely exceeded ten sentences, ran into seven pages. Ratface and I heard the paper rustle every time he turned a page. We counted them out loud. Mother called him several times. Sometimes he looked out of the window, rolling the pen over the page with his fingertips, his lips forming the words. Then he went on writing. After about an hour, he stood up and snapped the book shut, and suddenly his calm turned into euphoria. He danced into the kitchen, shuffled around us and lavished kisses on everyone. On Ratface and my crowns, and Mother full on the mouth.

Ratface and I expected some kind of miracle, a true story about how he had single-handedly captured four thieves that day, or pulled four children from the muddy bank of the River Scheldt. He sat down. Curbing her curiosity, Mother stood up to heat up his supper. And even though he didn't tell us anything that evening—of course we already knew it had something to do with the number four, or he wouldn't have written it in his notebook—we didn't mind. The memory of that moment, the four of us sitting in the kitchen together, the small windows steamed up from the food that had been heated twice, the smell of the bundles of herbs dangling from the cupboard knobs on strings, and Father and Mother both happy and relaxed (the perforated red ribbon around her ponytail), has always stayed with me. Only later, a few months before Ratface's death, did he tell me the story. It went as follows: he was to hang curtains in the office of one of the professors, and was deep in thought on how to go about it, when he turned to the west wall. He jumped. The whole wall was covered in writing and drawings. Several thick, curved black lines drawn on the wall crossed each other at regular intervals. The lowest curve, the largest, was a single arc running from one corner of the room to the other. The line of the large curve was crossed four times by a smaller one, which in turn was crossed eight times by the smallest curve. Each of the points of intersection was numbered, and the numbers never went higher than four. In Roman numerals and ordinary numbers. At the top, under the ceiling, was written in large letters: the Quaternity in History and Art History. Seeing this incomprehensible mural, which my father described as a revelation, had gone beyond sensory perception—even though he initially had no idea of its meaning, and was aware that it was a creation by a human being of flesh and blood, and no deity had been involved.

From what he saw there, and especially from the endless explanation given to him by the professor who had come in and found him squatting on the floor, he could only conclude that the shapes on the walls were a manifestation of his own emotions. It was the crowning confirmation of his long-standing obsession with the number four, drawn up and described on a giant scale. Professor Pekhart, for that was the name of the professor who had surprised him, brought out the chair from behind his desk, placed it behind my father's back and helped him onto it.

'Are you unwell?' he asked when he saw my father's ashen cheeks.

'No, professor,' he said. 'I'm sorry, professor.'

The professor helped him to his feet, then turned to the wall.

'What do you think of it?' Father recognized the tone of voice—It was that of someone who knew that what he had made was undeniably the work of an expert.

'It's ... overwhelming.'

'Do you understand what it means?' the professor asked in a friendly manner, knowing full well that the likelihood of a handyman fathoming his theory of the Quaternity by looking at a mural was practically nil. Even his colleagues barely grasped it, and dismissed anything their brilliant minds could not understand as pseudo-science. The professor smelled of eau de cologne. When Father turned his head to look at him, he noticed that a strand of hair above his forehead had a yellowish sheen.

'Tell you what,' the professor said, 'the curtains can wait until tomorrow. I'll explain it to you, though a couple of hours will hardly be enough time.'

He glanced at the clock. Father leaned back and spent the rest of the afternoon listening to Professor Pekhart.

I heard out his story with bated breath, until we were

rudely interrupted by Ratface storming into the room and demanding to know where his book about wolves was. He waited stubbornly. With a sigh, Father signalled to me that I should help him look. I stood up unwillingly. By the time we had finally found the book—under his own bed, of course—and ran back into the living room, Father wasn't there anymore.

'BUT SIR, WHY do we have to cram all these things into our heads?'

Roger interrupted my lesson about the capital cities of Europe. His way of constantly questioning everything drove me up the wall sometimes.

'Neither my father nor mother have ever been further than Ypres or Poperinge, and on Sundays, my mother goes straight home to milk the cows after Mass and my father only ever gets as far as the pub for a pint.'

'Quite a distance, if he has to crawl home,' Jef said.

We ignored the remark.

'Well, Roger. Maybe you will travel further than your parents one day, and see the whole wide world,' I said.

'Who, me? Why? Whaffor?'

'To look at churches and castles in other countries, perhaps. To see how people live there. Or to observe the wildlife.'

I thought of my childhood. Of the books Father brought us. Of the cupboard full of skulls and bones in my room. Of my brother.

'But I won't have the cash for that. And anyway, I don't give a damn about those things.'

Judging by the way his eyebrows twitched, he knew he should be watching his words.

'Honest, sir. All I want to do is milk the cows and work

the land. So why do I need to know the capitals of Europe, or who Napoleon was? And on Sundays, I want to go drinking, like Dad!'

I needed all my creativity to come up with an answer that would have a motivational effect on the obstinate lout.

'Well, Roger. Imagine that one day, you take over your father's farm ... '

He interrupted me enthusiastically.

'Oh, I will, sir! 'Cos luckily, I'm the oldest!' He laughed, sneering at Jef and Walter, who both had elder brothers.

'All right,' I continued. 'And now imagine you do, as you say, also take over that genial habit of your father's, namely drinking on Sundays.'

'Yes, naturally. Sometimes, I'm already allowed ... '

'That's enough, Roger,' I cut him short. 'As you know, however, no one on this planet is immortal. I'm sorry I have to say so, but one day, your parents will die.'

He fell silent at those words, looking downcast, and I could carry on talking uninterrupted.

'And your siblings will leave home one day, that's only natural.'

He was probably picturing it already.

'That means that you will be left on your own, with your cows, pigs and your beautiful, rolling fields of wheat.'

They were hanging on my every word.

'But I'll get married and have lots of children!' Roger said confidently.

'Ah. That's exactly what I was getting to, you took the words out of my mouth. Don't misunderstand me, there's nothing wrong with things like cows and pigs and rolling wheat fields. But it can get lonely if you don't have anyone to share them with. So yes, you are indeed very likely to marry and have children. That's correct. But imagine you fall in love with a pretty girl but can't really get to know her—you only ever see her in church on Sundays, and her father and brothers are very protective of her, because she's so lovely.'

Stony silence.

'Just like Giselle Blankaert,' Jef said seriously.

'That fat, ugly carrot-top?' Walter blurted out, and it was all I could do to prevent Jef from swinging his fist at him by cracking my ruler down on the desk with all my strength. I noticed it had dented the smooth surface, but at least the boys were quiet and I could continue my story.

'So there you are, spending your Sundays drinking in the pub, and the girls won't be there … but who will?'

'Their father and brothers,' Marcus said.

'Exactly! And in pubs, plenty of things are discussed over a pint. Just think, Roger, how impressed her father or brother will be if you can tell them who Napoleon was, and why he was so important. Or if you know that Antwerp is not in Germany. The man will go home feeling that Roger Malfait is a damned clever bloke who will go far in life, and that he wouldn't mind his daughter bringing him home.'

Roger thought about this, and said, 'My father always says you shouldn't choose a pretty woman because you'll never have her completely to yourself. As long as her legs are straight, he always says.'

'My father says bandy legs are better,' Walter said. "'Cos then it won't hurt when she squeezes them together.'

I realized that my pedagogic moment had already come to an end again, but enjoyed the look of admiration in Marcus's eyes.

THE NEWS THAT farmer Verschoppen was the owner of my house had lodged itself into my mind. Mustering all my courage, I decided to alert the rightful owner himself to my mould-infested bedroom. I chose an early Sunday morning as the best chance of meeting him sober and perhaps even in an accommodating mood, given the promising prospect of beer at the Pumphouse. With that reassuring thought in mind, I wrapped up well, locked the front door and set out in the direction of the village square. When I walked past the pub, Victor was already at his post. I squared my shoulders and flung my legs forward further than usual. I must have looked like a marching soldier, I thought with embarrassment as I turned into Vlamertinge Road. I only slowed down once I was safely out of Victor's sight. Past Forest Lane. The castle to my right, still wreathed in mist, the pond in front of it full of swans and white water lilies. The gate was open. On the fringe of the village, the path narrowed and the fields and meadows of Elverdinge stretched out before me. Not far now. The sky seemed to clear a little when I turned into Hospital Lane.

I hesitated at the drive. This was Buck's territory. I had a perfect view, however. The drive was as straight as an arrow, I would be able to spot a charging dog at once and still have time to scramble up one of the pollard willows.

They looked old and decayed, large pieces of bark dangled from them, and they had holes as big as my torso. I walked on. Still no Buck bounding toward me. No rattling chains, either. A little owl shooting out of a hole in one of the willows startled me more than I would have liked. Barking: angry, but distant. The front door was already opening. Marcus appeared in the doorway, carrying his sketchbook under his arm. He looked at me in surprise. Then his mother appeared behind him. Her light brown hair gathered in a bun high on the back of her head. She was wearing a white blouse and a dragonfly-blue belt around her waist. She put her hands on his shoulders, her lips in a tight, desperate line. I stopped a few metres in front of them. The barking continued, muffled, but urgent and vicious. I expected farmer Verschoppen to burst out of the open stable doors, his hardened body stride over the yard toward me and run me through with a pitchfork like a dried-up cowpat.

'Good morning,' I said.

'Good morning,' they said in unison.

'Please come in.'

'We haven't met,' she said, extending her hand to me. 'I'm Godaleva. Marcus's mother.'

Godaleva. What a beautiful name, I thought. As soft on the tongue as a slice of ripe pear.

'I am David Verbocht, the new teacher.' I said.

She fiddled with her belt. Marcus inched backward. I winked at him in passing as I followed his mother over the beautiful tiled floor. The skirt did nothing to hide her voluptuous behind. Marcus almost stepped on my heels. The place was full of ornaments, vases and other, smaller knick-knacks. It looked like a huge doll's house.

'Do sit down,' she said, showing me to an armchair in a corner at the window.

I was still braced for humiliation, certain that farmer Verschoppen would make an appearance and ignore me mercilessly. But for some reason, Godaleva made me feel safe. Just like Marcus. His delicate frame looked more supple than it did when he stood on the playground watching the other boys' games from his place at the wall.

'Cup of coffee?'

As she walked to the kitchen, Marcus sat down in the armchair opposite me. He looked me up and down, trying hard to hide his curiosity.

'What are you drawing?' I asked.

'A ladybird.'

He sprang up from his seat, grabbed the jar standing on the table and shoved it under my nose. I spotted the insect in between the different shades of green. He had even put some greenflies in with it.

'I know, I know,' he said in a pedantic tone, 'I'll set it free again when I'm finished with it.'

Godaleva came in, carrying a steaming tray. She had tied an apron around her waist.

'Mother, may I have a biscuit, please?' Marcus asked.

She nodded and offered me one, too. I nibbled at the biscuit like a tame rabbit. The crushing sound it made between my molars irritated me. Her hands were resting on the edge of the table. They looked shapely, and the fingers betrayed sensitivity. I didn't want to tell her and Marcus that I had actually come to see Verschoppen.

'I expected Buck to welcome me,' I said to Marcus.

Marcus answered that Buck was locked up in the stable as punishment for biting four chicks to death the day before.

'And it wasn't the first time, either,' Godaleva sighed.

'If he ever does it again, Father will shoot him,' Marcus added. His voice was choked with emotion, biscuit crumbs stuck to his lips. It seemed to me that putting down an Alsatian would be quite a job, but Verschoppen would probably do it without batting an eyelid.

'We'll make sure the chicks are safely locked up,' she said soothingly.

I could tell Marcus was not completely reassured.

Then she looked at me.

'Do you always take a walk on Sundays?'

'Not just on Sundays,' I answered. 'Elverdinge is full of country lanes worth exploring. It really is a beautiful part of the country, with a character all its own. And sometimes, on a very clear day, you can see the outlines of the hills in the distance. Picturesque.'

I felt like an idiot, prattling on to a woman over whom powerful rivals would have waged wars in the past. I had to get away, and cursed the fact that the farmer of the house wasn't home, so I could have told him about my mould wars in private.

She must have noticed my unease, as she asked me whether I was interested in seeing the farm. It was Sunday, the farmhands wouldn't be there, she added with a look at Marcus, and he nodded.

We went to the stable behind the house. A furry bumblebee bumped against my shoulder and got stuck on the fabric of my pullover. I carefully brushed the insect off. In the stable, long wisps of cobwebs hung down from the rafters. It looked mysterious, like a woven mist. Marcus stopped and pointed at a closed stable door.

'Buck's in there. Father told me not to open the door,' he said glumly.

'Not even to show him to me?'

'I don't know. I can't ask him, he's not home.'

The barking turned into whining. Claws were scrabbling against the lower part of the door.

'I'll come back another time,' I said.

I would have to, unless I happened to bump into Verschoppen somewhere else, as I hadn't been able to raise the subject of the mould. Marcus didn't seem to believe it though, and went to the door after all. He slid across the bolt of the top half and it swung open. Buck immediately tried to climb out. I could see his paws on the edge of the lower door, and his hairy head appeared every time he leapt up. Marcus waved me closer. If Buck took a running leap, he'd easily clear the door, I thought. But cautiously glancing over the edge, I saw the rope around his neck. It was too tight.

'He mustn't get too excited or he'll strangle himself with that rope,' I said.

Marcus never took his eyes from his dog, who paid for his attempts to leap over the door with heavy panting and a rattling cough. I could see his inner struggle, but was also acutely aware of the danger lurking in the sinister figure of his father.

'Perhaps your father will come back soon, and you can tell him,' I tried to reassure him.

But Marcus, defiant, slid open the bolt of the lower door. Buck licked his face as he kneeled, searching for the rope with quick fingers.

Then we heard her call. She waved to us, standing beside the house with the sun behind her. Marcus went on fumbling at the rope, but couldn't loosen it. He muttered something to Buck, who had calmed down a bit. He could hardly breathe, but his tail still wagged faintly every time Marcus's hand stroked the fur on his neck. The whites of his eyes were streaked with delicate red lines. Her voice grew louder. I tried to help Marcus, but my fingers were too clumsy. Hooves thundered over the cobbled drive at full speed. Then they stopped, and we heard the snorting of the horse behind our backs. Still in the saddle, Verschoppen ordered Marcus to go indoors immediately. He dismounted and came into the stable. Grabbing Buck's head, he took out a knife and flicked it open. When he was finished, he turned to me, still holding the knife. His body blocked out the light. Buck hobbled outside, his tail between his legs.

'Mr Verbocht was taking a walk and decided to pay us a visit,' Godaleva said behind his back.

He snapped the knife shut. She came into the stable and stood next to him. Behind their backs, the outdoors beckoned.

'Come. Let's go in and have coffee,' she said. He didn't move.

'I was actually hoping to meet you,' I said to him, realizing too late that Godaleva would know I had lied.

We stood facing each other.

'Come,' she said again. 'We can talk inside.'

She turned round and walked away. To my relief, he also turned and went to the stallion pawing the ground, its coat soaked with sweat. Taking the horse by the reins, he whispered something to it and led it away. I hurried after her, though I didn't much feel like going inside again.

Marcus wasn't there. We awaited Verschoppen's arrival in silence. I nibbled at another biscuit, a cup of coffee on the table before me. Remembering from earlier that I took milk and sugar with my coffee, she had placed the china jug and sugar bowl in front of me. I watched her hands, the gentle slope from her knuckles down to her wrists, the slightly tanned skin. An occasional blonde hair catching the sunlight. He came in. She poured coffee for him, too. Black. Her hand was steady.

'Where's Marcus?' he asked.

'Upstairs,' she said.

The cup looked fragile in his fist. His finger was too large for the handle.

'What did you want of me?' he asked. I didn't feel like talking about the mould, especially in Godaleva's presence. It's not the most appetizing life form in the universe.

'Mr Vantomme tells me you're the owner of the house I'm renting,' I said.

'That's right.'

The hot edge of the cup stuck to my lip. I tried not to show the pain.

'I was a little surprised, since he was the one who gave me the keys and to whom I pay the rent.'

'He lives close by and doesn't have anything better to do.'

Godaleva stood up. The subject didn't interest her, but she did give me an apologetic look before disappearing in the hall. A moment later, I heard her footsteps on the stairs.

'Is that why you came? To find out whether the house is mine?'

A door slammed shut upstairs. The muffled voices of mother and son. Relieved that Godaleva had left, I seized my chance.

'Actually, I went to see Mr Vantomme to ask whether he could send someone over to scrub the mould off my wall.'

'Mould?'

'Yes.'

'Can't you do that yourself?'

'I've tried, twice, but it keeps coming back. I'm afraid that other measures need to be taken.'

'Such as?'

'That is up to you, the landlord, to decide.'

He had finished his coffee and poured himself another one.

'I'll give you a bucket of fungicide.'

He stood up and went out of the door. I tossed back the dregs of my coffee and followed him to a small shed. Pouring the poison into a bucket at my feet, he told me it was a new product. The stuff was a slimy green colour, and its stench was already turning my stomach.

'Here you are.'

He nodded at the bucket standing between us.

'Have a nice Sunday, schoolmaster.'

And he was gone. I would have liked to say goodbye to Marcus and Godaleva, but decided against it. Carrying the heavy bucket past the farmhouse, I saw Verschoppen standing in the living room, holding his cup at his chest.

The stuff sloshed around in the bucket and sometimes over its dented edge, staining my Sunday trousers and shoes. It frothed with foul, yellowish bubbles. I trudged along laboriously, trying to spill as little as possible, when it struck me this was the second time I was carrying a heavy load around like a mule. This time, however, I was unexpectedly given a hand. Victor came up to me as I lugged toward him. I put down the bucket because I thought he wanted to talk to me, and he picked it up.

'All that hauling buckets and coal scuttles isn't fitting for a teacher,' he said.

I was grateful to him, and said so. But at the same moment, the cracking of bone and his callously gazing down at the bodies in the street flashed through my mind again.

'What is this stuff?' he asked, nodding at the bucket.

'Fungicide. For the mould in my bedroom. A new product, farmer Verschoppen said.'

'Verschoppen? I see. It'll be all right, then.'

We walked on together. I wanted to ask him about his job at the pub. How he had come by it. And what had become of the two men. And whether that kind of thing happened often. But I kept quiet.

'There you go,' he said, placing the bucket on my front step.

'Thank you. Please come in.'

'Another time,' he said.

He turned and walked away. I watched him for a bit with mixed feelings. His form slowly shrinking into the distance, his clothes the same colour as the cobbles he was walking on.

WE HAD BOTH brought our pocket knives and the sawn-off handle of a broom, to slash and thrash our way through the thorns and thistles. I knew the path turned off at the end. It ran in a loop, and if you followed it, you ended up where you started. So we decided to carry on straight ahead at the bend. At first, it almost seemed as if someone had gone before us. A narrow, almost invisible track wound its way between the tree trunks and bushes. I felt a pang of disappointment, mixed with surprise. We weren't the first, though I couldn't remember ever having seen anyone else in the woods. After following the track for a while, I realized it wasn't a man-made path put a game trail, made by animals on their way to their favourite foraging ground or drinking place. Occasionally, the tracks spread out, especially around beech trees, oaks and horse chestnuts. Churned-up soil close to the trunk exposed the roots. Piles of dung and droppings were scattered around like miniature hills.

After a couple of hour's walking, Ratface was hungry, but I wanted to find a nice place before stopping for lunch. The undergrowth was tough, the trees mostly spindly saplings. I wanted to have our picnic under the vaulted canopy of an old tree—the most beautiful place in a forest. Where you could feel the wood itself take a deep breath, and where the young trees and sprawling thicket kept a reverential distance from the ancient tree that allowed nothing in the shade of its branches but a soft, decaying carpet of leaves and humus. Of course I couldn't be sure we'd even find such a place, but I gambled on it.

Ratface's stomach rumbled, but he didn't complain. He was looking around all the time, peering into the air and at the ground. I knew he spotted more than I did and would only alert me to things that were really worth seeing. Sometimes he'd squat, take a stick and poke it into something—droppings, probably, or owl pellets—or quickly flip over a leaf, looking for a beetle that had scuttled underneath. I would usually retrace my steps to find out what he was doing. Not today. I walked on. Sometimes he called me, but started following me again when I didn't react, looking over his shoulder now and again. For a boy his age, the wood was still a mysterious and frightening place, a mist-shrouded fairy-tale forest that could easily hide creatures no other human being had ever seen before.

'A monter,' he said.

'What's that?'

'It's an animal as big as a bull that lives in the woods. Instead of horns, it has sharp canines.'

'Doesn't exist.'

'Does, too! And it has four eyes.'

'Ratface, it doesn't exist! It's in none of the books!'

'Even so, I've read about it!'

I searched my mind for an animal with a similar-sounding name. Perhaps he had misread the word. Or maybe he simply meant monster. Not that that was likely, though—Ratface never misread a word.

'It's a carnivore,' he said, proud of having remembered the term and being able to use it.

'And its coat is soft. Like that of mink.'

I couldn't find a single animal name in the archive of my

brain that sounded anything like it.

'There aren't any animals with more than two eyes.'

'Yes there are! Spiders! Some spiders even have eight eyes! And there are plenty of even stranger things in nature you know nothing about,' he added heatedly. "Cos I've read a lot more books about them than you have. So I know more.'

That was true. It was all he ever did.

'Tuataras have three eyes! There's one on the top of their heads!'

'That's as may be, but there's no such thing as a monter!'

I was getting irritated. Ratface, who was walking about a metre behind me, stopped abruptly. My annoyance melted away when I saw his trembling lower lip. He hung his head and stared at the tops of his shoes. I thought of all the things I had promised him the night before, the wildlife we would see, and felt guilty. I went up to him and put my arm around his shoulders.

'You walk so fast and I'm hungry,' he said.

'Then we'll eat something, here and now.'

I opened my rucksack and crouched down to take out the lunchboxes with the sandwiches, and the two canteens. We sat face to face among the ferns, a few metres away from the game trail. That way, we might get to see an unsuspecting animal going about its daily business.

'Don't you agree that sandwiches always taste best eaten outdoors?'

He nodded, put his finger in his mouth to lick off a small dab of butter he had noticed on it. We continued our meal in silence, listening to the sounds of the forest. Only now I was really paying attention to them, did I hear it: water. Gently murmuring. I stood up and walked toward the sound. Ratface chewed on unhurriedly, washing down each bite with a gulp from his canteen. I stopped, turned my head in the direction of the faint babbling, went on. High above my head, a startled wood pigeon flew up, wings clapping together in the air. Then, after only about fifty paces, I arrived at the brook. It was a deep-set, winding little stream. We would easily be able to leap over it.

When I returned, Ratface had gone. He had put his lunch box and canteen back in the rucksack. I called his name, let the echo die down, called again. More startled fluttering of birds. The undergrowth rustled, no more than a dozen metres away from me. Perhaps he was hiding behind a bush, watching me with a grin on his face. I shouted at the top of my voice. He answered, from far away, that I should come and see. I saw him wave between the slender trunks and ran toward him. He pointed at a bulky object at his feet.

'A dead roe deer. Hasn't been dead long. Maybe a day,' I said.

Flies landed on the clotted blood, on the bowels spilling out of its belly. I crouched down to examine the carcass. It was an adult animal, a male, even. No natural enemies.

'A hunter?' Ratface asked, as baffled as I was.

'A hunter wouldn't have left it behind.'

'There's no predator strong enough here to kill an adult roebuck,' I said.

'Maybe it was ill?' Ratface asked. He looked over his shoulder, perhaps to make sure his four-eyed monter with the mink-soft coat wasn't around.

'It doesn't look ill. Strapping build. Lovely shiny coat. No broken legs or shot wounds,' I said, inspecting the animal more closely. Its belly had been torn open, not cut. It could only have been done by powerful fangs. Slowly lifting its hind leg, I could see deep into the hollow of its belly.

'The vital organs have gone.'

'Can we cut off its head and take it with us? Then we can

bury it at home. I want the skull for my rack,' Ratface said.

I looked at the fur of its neck, still glistening wet. It could be done. We had our knives with us. But the thought of beheading the animal, dead though it was, filled me with deep disgust. Nor was I keen on the prospect of lugging home the bleeding head in my rucksack with our food and drink.

'I can do it, if you're too scared,' Ratface said. Sensing my hesitation, he had already opened his knife.

'I'm not scared, it's not that. But I think we shouldn't do it out of respect for the deer.'

'It's dead already.'

'That doesn't mean we have to mutilate it even more.'

'So do you want to bury it?' Ratface asked.

I shook my head and said we should leave it where it was, and perhaps later, once all the flesh had gone and the skull was bleached, we could come back to collect it. He liked the idea. We wove some sticks around the carcass to mark the spot. Walking back to the place we'd left the rucksack, I was still wondering how the animal had been killed. But I didn't want to think about it any more. We had to hurry up.

'I've found a brook,' I said.

'We still haven't seen a single animal,' Ratface said.

'Maybe on our way back. Many forest animals are nocturnal and only come out at dusk. You know that.'

It had been a dry summer, and even now, in autumn, there was little rain. I jumped first. I don't know why, but the thump of my feet coming down on the soil reminded me of the sound of my father's axe hitting the chopping block—the muffled thud that went straight through the flesh and vertebrae of the chickens' feathered necks. I pulled Ratface to his feet after his leap, banishing the image of the decapitated chicken from my mind.

'Not far now,' I said.

Noticing a suspicious silence behind me, I turned around. Ratface was staring straight ahead. He looked like a statue carved from candle wax. I was afraid he would faint and roll down backward into the stream, and quickly grabbed his arm.

'What's the matter?' I asked, instinctively whispering.

He didn't move. I followed his gaze, peered through the trees, but saw nothing.

'What have you seen?'

He lifted his arm and pointed. No movement. No sound. Only the rustle of leaves in the treetops. And the faint babbling of the water in the brook behind us.

'I can't see anything, Ratface,' I said, after we had stared for at least a minute, 'and I'm dying for a pee.'

Still tense, I walked to a tree about ten metres away. Ratface stayed where he was, his eyes fixed on the spot he had pointed to. Leaning against the tree with one hand, I used the other to aim the jet of piss at the bark to flush out beetles and spiders. Then I heard his scream. The scene unfolded in chilling slow-motion. I jerked my head round, and in the corner of my eye saw a formless silhouette breaking away from the shadows of the bushes and tearing toward Ratface. I took a running leap and dove in between Ratface and the beast. I didn't feel it biting my arm. The teeth clamping shut around the bone. I didn't feel it, though I saw blood. The frenzy of my resistance and the strength of my fingers tightening around its throat must have made the beast abandon its plan of mauling Ratface. No time, no free hand to take out my knife. But Ratface had rushed to my aid, hitting the wolf, or dog, or cross between the two, with his stick, giving it a good, hard wallop that forced it to let go of my arm and sink its teeth into the stick. Just enough time for me to thrust my hand into my trouser pockets, and, not having found the knife, turn over quickly and scramble to my feet. But sensing the threat, the animal let go of the stick and turned on me again, jaws snapping shut just beside my shoulder. I fell. On my belly. I turned over, blinded by a red haze, and screamed to Ratface that he should run away. Lying on my back, I started to feel faint. The wolf-dog, or dog-wolf, hesitated for an instant, lifting its pale blue eyes to Ratface, who had jumped back over the brook. I seized its muzzle with both hands and snapped it shut, feeling a rush of power as the fangs pierced the tongue and I heard the beast whine, felt its body shudder in pain. Blood and drool on my forehead, in my eyes. It whipped its head from side to side, raging with pain. I knew I wouldn't be able to hold on for much longer and was hoping Ratface had had enough time to get away, perhaps climb a tree, when to my horror, I saw him still standing there.

'Ratface, run! Run!'

I screamed. I was losing my grip, my fingers slipping off its muzzle. Ratface stood there. Crying. Stamping his feet. Then, out of nowhere, a chain around its neck, a strong jolt, a gunshot. At point-blank range. Shards of bone sprayed over my chest.

'That was Zaebos,' she said, bending over me. I saw black hair through the red haze, and thinking I was being beset by yet another monster, tried to fend it off with my arms. She pushed her arm under my shoulders and pulled me to my feet. Ratface was already standing beside me. I was tired, and wanted to lie down on the leaves again. Pain pulsed through my arm in waves. I heard the swish of her belt as she whisked it from her waist and tied off my arm. She said she would take us to her house, where she would dress the wound. Her arm was around my waist. She was a little shorter than me, her hair lank and smooth, a hint of darkness in her skin.

'Thank you,' I muttered.

'Your flies are open,' she said. I tried to button them up with my right hand. Embarrassed that I wasn't able to, I wanted to ask Ratface to help me, but she stopped, crouched down and did it herself. She only lived a few hundred metres from the spot where Zaebos had attacked me. He had been the leader of her pack, but then he had turned vicious and bitten two young dogs to death before running away. That had been three days earlier. She had looked for him, then tried to lure him with boiled pheasant—his favourite food—when she hadn't been able to find him. She had known he had watched her from a distance. Ratface told her about the dead deer, its ripped-open belly and the heap of intestines on the ground. She listened as she slid open the bolt on the garden gate. I was still leaning on her arm. There were two dogs behind the gate.

'Cali and Scox,' she said. 'Mother and son. Zaebos was the father.' We walked past the dogs. Afraid, Ratface went ahead of us quickly, tripping over his own feet. In the kitchen, she gave him a glass of water and an apple, then pulled up a chair and helped me sit down. Her name was Myrtha. She fetched another chair, sat down and carefully lifted up my arm. It was the same one that had been scalded all those years ago. The skin was as smooth as soap in patches, with bunched-up, knobbly edges. She wiped off the blood with a cloth and traced the wound with her fingertips, pressing gently to feel how deep the bite went. Then she turned her upper body, pulled open a drawer and took out a first-aid box. I saw the bulge of her breast under her pullover. She opened the box with one hand. It was full of bandages, needles, scissors and other things.

'Shouldn't he go to a real doctor?' Ratface asked. He turned his eyes away from my arm and looked at the dogs, who were whining and pressing their noses against the screen door of the kitchen.

'I've done this before,' she said.

Her composure, her apparent familiarity with what had just happened, gave me complete confidence in her. While she was making the preparations, she told Ratface that he could go outside to the dogs if he liked. Scox was particularly fond of playing. He was only twelve months old. She pointed out a red ball lying in the grass. But Ratface didn't want to. The traces of his tears were still visible on his face. I winked at him, hiding my pain, when she started. I was proud of him. He placed the core of his apple on the table. Bending down low over my arm, Myrtha draped her hair to one side of her face, away from the wound. Every time the needle and thread slipped through the flesh, I felt a tingling sting in my forearm. Inhaling the scent drifting up from her hair, I felt warm and drowsy inside. When she was finished, she bandaged my arm. Then she poured us tea and put a bowl of biscuits on the table. Ratface grabbed one, took a tentative bite and then shoved it into his mouth in one go. In the silence of the kitchen, we heard his molars pulverize the crumbs.

'I'm sorry about Zaebos,' I said.

Ratface, who had decided to go out after all, was throwing the ball in the back garden. It bounced off the fence and shot up into the air. With an impressive leap, Cali or Scox—I could hardly tell them apart—snatched the ball out of the air.

She shook her head. 'He was a gun dog. He was old and worn out.'

I looked at a grainy photograph on the wall, a man leaning on the handle of his rifle, a dog with pitch-black eyes staring into the lens as if its prey were hiding behind it. A dark pile of dead game like a hillock behind them.

'That's my husband. And yes, that is Zaebos,' she said, seeing the question in my eyes.

'We lived in South Africa at the time. They went big-game hunting together.'

I felt at ease in her presence. She was silent for a time, as if her mind had become foggy with memories.

'He's dead,' she said.

She told me he'd been a soldier, and that he had fought in the Boer War. Ratface was now running from one end of the garden to the other, the dogs in wild pursuit, lured by the ball. In another room, a clock struck four. We still had the journey home ahead of us.

'This path,' she pointed to the front of the house, 'runs round the furthest part of the woods, then cuts straight through it and joins the footpath. You know it, I suppose.'

I nodded. Pain shot through my arm and shoulder as I stood up. She held out her hand. I felt her skin, the calluses. I didn't want to leave. I wanted to stay at her kitchen table. She would light some candles when it got dark. Show me more photographs. Drink tea. Tell me what the scent was, rising from her hair. South African flowers? Cali and Scox would lie at our feet. An indefinable atmosphere dominated this kitchen, the smell of adventure. Something that didn't exist at home. But we had to go back. I let go of her hand and called Ratface. He shook her hand wildly, still fired up from playing with the dogs.

'Come back sometime,' she said to him. 'I have a surprise for you.'

Thrilled at the invitation, Ratface and I promised we would. Outside, she repeated her directions—as she pointed down the path we should follow I watched her breasts again, which, now that Myrtha stood before me with her arm raised, looked smaller than before—and said we could make it before dark if we walked briskly.

IT WAS THE worst nightmare I had ever had. I was being chased by green, masked creatures. Hordes of them. Running through the undergrowth as fast as I could, I zigzagged between tree trunks and leapt over ditches, plunging my hands into thistles and thorns. There was a sharp smell in the air. I had never smelled it before. I ran on, coughing and hacking. Slime dribbled down my chin. They were so close to me now I could hear their screams—or rather, growls. Like dogs. Not humans, in any case. I reached a bridge. Down below, I saw white water lilies on the clear, starlit surface. I leaned on the edge of the bridge, and bending forward, felt the bricks give way at my knees. The non-humans had almost caught up with me. The growlers. I could hardly catch my breath. The air turned my lungs to ashes, scorched my insides. But down there, it looked safe. Under the water. Beneath the water lilies. I jumped. My stomach dissolved in tingling. And I went on falling.

My fingers painfully gripped the frame of my sleeping trough. The room was spinning. I couldn't tell whether my eyes were open or closed. My breath came in gasps. Until it slowly dawned on me where I was, and I could see through the attic window that it was still dark outside. The bed was awfully clammy. I was drenched. And that smell. It smelled distinctly different from the stuff I had smeared on the walls several hours ago. Like a mixture of sweat and curdled milk. I crawled out of bed, pulled off the sheets and sniffed at them. To my shame and disgust, my suspicion was confirmed. I, David Verbocht, twenty-two years old and teacher of Year Six, had wet my bed.

FATHER SPENT MORE and more time in the shed. It was the third weekday evening in a row he was still sitting there long after dark. Mother sent me to fetch him. I saw the flickering light through the window. Curious, I walked over the cobbled path to the shed, taking care not to fall over a spade or rake lying around. I knocked at the door, heard thumping and shuffling, fabric brushing over boards, a chair being banged down. I knocked again. He didn't seem to hear me, so I opened the door myself. Father was standing on a chair, his back turned to me. He had painted one wall of the shed black, then scribbled all over it with chalk: undulating lines. Roman numerals. Titles. Dates. Short pieces of text. He was holding his notebook in his left hand and frantically copying its contents onto the painted wall. Standing on the chair in his work clothes, chalk streaks on his face and trouser legs, he looked every inch the handyman I knew so well. But the things he was writing and drawing on the wall did not fit the picture, and standing in the doorway, I wondered whether he had lost his mind. Perhaps he had hit his head at work, or inhaled too many toxic fumes while painting the inside walls of the new university buildings. I slammed the door behind me, feeling a stream of cold air hit my ankles. He turned round with a start, the chalk in his hands hovering in mid-air without touching the surface, like a magic wand snapped in half.

'David, you couldn't have come at a better time. Hold on a moment, it's almost finished. A real work of art, don't you think? But it's much more than that. It is pure genius, though I say so myself.'

He turned round and went on scribbling. I walked to the middle of the floor and stood facing the wall. Though I recognized some things I'd learnt from Mother's history lessons, most of the terms—and the concept of dividing history into four repeating periods—were new to me. At that moment, my father put a large full stop after the word 'crisis', pressing down hard on the chalk and twisting it back and forth like a key that wouldn't turn in the lock. It rained fragments of chalk. Wiping his hands on his working trousers, he leapt from the chair. Then he stood beside me, examining his work of art with a boyish beam on his face. He put his arm around my shoulder.

'I've known it for years,' he said. 'Ever since Henri arrived and I started thinking about the magical number four. From that moment on, I felt there was more to the number than I had realized. Much more than just the facts we used to rattle down at the table. Do you remember?'

'Of course,' I said, not without a pang of nostalgia.

'But that was just the beginning of the mystery. I didn't realize at the time that I had embarked on a kind of quest,' he said. 'I was just going round in circles, following my intuition. I sensed there had to be more to it, but couldn't put my finger on it. The reason is staggeringly simple: I was ignorant. But not anymore! Thanks to Professor Pekhart! I went to his office to hang up some curtains, and what I saw there—well, I've told you before. I felt like a little child seeing lightning strike close by for the first time!'

He was shouting so loudly his voice rebounded from the wooden walls and echoed around the room. It was hurting my ears.

'I can hear you, Dad!' I shouted back.

Then I heard footsteps. I must have been out for some time—too long for Mother's liking, and she came in without knocking, holding Ratface by the hand. Father was delighted to have his whole family gathered around him at the very moment, after years of struggle, that his obsession came to fruition and he was finally able to explain his quest for the magic of the number four. He behaved as if his family had lived in hardship and cold for years, until now, at last, he was bringing them fire. He placed three chairs next to each other and invited us to sit down. I could tell Mother was ill at ease. She had never seen Father like this. Ratface loved it, he couldn't wait to hear what Father was so excited about.

'What I am about to tell you and will try to explain, is a theory about art and history that is called the Quaternity. A theory propagated by Professor Pekhart of Ghent University, who, I am proud to say, has become a close friend of mine.'

Ratface clapped his hands prematurely. I gave him a shove. Father dragged a table out of a dark corner of the shed. On the table were four objects: the scale model of a building, a figurine, a small painting and a musical instrument that resembled a shepherd's flute.

'These objects represent the four greatest historical art forms,' he said. 'Architecture, sculpture, painting and music.'

Mother nodded. I could tell she was paying close attention. She crossed her legs. The white flesh in the crook of her knee above her stocking was criss-crossed with purple lines like the veins in blue cheese. Ratface was sitting between us, hands resting on the knee-pads of his oversized trousers.

'You might not understand it at first,' Father said. 'It took me a long time to fathom how powerful the system was. And many notebooks.' He smiled at Mother, hesitated.

'I'm not sure where to begin,' he said pensively.

'Perhaps you should start with the objects on the table,' Mother encouraged him. She cast a quick glance in our direction. The teacher in her had discovered the educational value of the situation.

'Quite, yes,' Father said. He turned round, picked up the model, wavered for a moment and put it back.

'Actually, I should explain something else first—to give you a point of reference,' he said, with a hopeful look on his face.

'I'm waiting,' Ratface said.

Then my father started talking. He made ample use of the drawings on the shed wall. I watched a procession of beetles and woodlice crawl in and out of the gap between the floor and the wall. The tough, withered birch bracket he used to pin his notes on gave off a strange, yellowish glow. What he told us made me realize how much he had learned, all by himself, and of course with Professor Pekhart's help. He said that history, and therefore the future, was based on a division by four, and pointed in turn to 1: crisis, 2: construction; 3: completion; 4: expansion. This pattern kept re-emerging. Across civilisations. And within them, too. Each quaternity builds on what went before. He pointed to the numbers on the wall. A crisis, the period of Western history we were in at that moment, he said, is dominated by dissolution. World views that have already run to seed will eventually perish, as in a crisis, everyone is wrapped up in their own secular little life. Eventually, it leads to chaos. But frightened people look for a way out. Something new to hold on to. Thus a new ideal is born from chaos. That ideal is again constructed, completed and expanded. And followed by another crisis.

'What has all that got to do with the things on the table?' Ratface asked.

'Well,' Father said, pleased with the question, 'each of the four periods has its own prominent art form.' He picked up the flute and said, 'In times of crisis, the most important art form is music. But in times of construction, architecture is most crucial.' He picked up the model. 'For that is the time to separate the newly discovered ideal from the world around it, to create a new space in which it can be experienced. Take the cloisters, for instance. The most important art form in a completion period is sculpture. And during an expansion period, it is painting.'

He picked up the picture and, holding it with both hands, rested it against his chin.

Mother understood little of what he said. I even less. Ratface was getting bored.

'It's all a bit, um, vague,' Mother said cautiously. I could tell she didn't want to discourage Father, or hurt him. 'And difficult.'

Father sighed.

'Yes. It's very difficult,' he admitted. 'But it really is ingenious. It provides an insight into history, and therefore into the future. It's a way of understanding the world, based on the number four.' He was mumbling now and we could barely understand him. Mother stood up and hugged him. She kissed him. Ratface clapped his hands with abandon. Mother whispered something into Father's ear. He smiled. Then he suddenly grabbed her round the waist, and they danced around the shed, humming and whirling. To crisis period music, I thought.

FATHER STORME WAS at the door. It had been an exhausting day. I was finding it more and more difficult to keep the boys under control. The most ordinary things—a glob of snot or a sudden burp—disrupted and delayed the lessons. Marcus and Roger understood the subject matter. The others didn't really care. All in all, I didn't feel like company, but let him in out of politeness. There was a drizzle outside. I don't know if his wet cassock was the reason, but his mood was anything but sunny. I could tell from his grumpy hello.

'Would you like some coffee?'

'Humph.'

I went to the kitchen to fill the kettle. I knew he would be snooping in the pile of essays lying on the table that I had been marking. He didn't even bother to stop reading when I returned with the coffee cups. It was Roger's essay, titled 'The Crusaders Fighting the Saracen'. He snorted and sipped his coffee without raising his head. Then he put the essay back on the top of the pile and gave me a searching look.

'Mr Verbocht, it pains me that I have not yet been able to welcome you in my church.'

I felt put on the spot. And in my own home, too.

'You must understand that a teacher should always set a good example.'

He took a large gulp of his coffee.

'Father,' I said, 'of course I want to set a good example. That goes without saying. In my lessons, I dedicate an appropriate amount of time to the virtues and rituals of the Catholic faith.'

At the word 'rituals', his eyebrows shot up and a shadow of aversion crossed his face.

'I do not doubt it,' he said. 'But words alone are not enough. A man is distinguished by his deeds, above all.'

'That is true,' I said.

'So you realize you are not setting a good example if you don't attend Mass every Sunday?'

'I prefer being true to my own beliefs.'

'And what beliefs would those be?' he asked curtly. It was not the best moment for broaching the subject. It was dark. There was a drizzle, and neither of us felt like having this conversation. But it was time I shared my views on religious practice with the priest. It was something I had given a lot of thought from an early age. I came straight to the point.

'Forgive me for saying so, Father, but I see religion as a leaking lifeboat for the ill and frail. To me, a mentally healthy person is someone who believes in himself and finds strength in himself, without the help of an enforced, compulsive belief in an external power. Only a well-balanced human being can be of use to others.'

His jaw dropped. He stared at me for a few moments, probably wondering whether he had misheard me.

'That is the reason I don't attend Mass on Sundays,' I concluded my short explanation.

Recovering from his surprise with difficulty, he eventually managed to compose himself.

'But you are the teacher of Year Six! Catholic boys each and every one, who go to Mass with their fathers and mothers every Sunday. Some of them are even altar boys!'

'I'm aware of that, Father.'

His eyebrows knitted together. I could have sworn they grew longer and thicker until they fused into a single bar of bushy hair.

'Elverdinge is a closely knit, Catholic community,' he said. 'This year alone, three parishioners have left for the Congo to convert Negroes.'

I didn't know what to say to that.

'How on earth did you get this job?'

I didn't want to tell him my father had arranged it.

'The usual procedure,' I lied.

He stared at me in astonishment.

'So shall we never see you in church?' he asked.

I shook my head. There was a silence as the last remnant of light rapidly fled from the narrow slits his eyes had become. He stood up, marched to the door and slammed it behind him. I heard the patter of raindrops on the cobbles. There was a sudden draught in the living room. The outside air that had been drawn in through the open door chilled my ankles. I realized the conversation was likely to have consequences, but felt strangely relieved all the same. I wasn't afraid—a man who daren't speak his own mind is only half a man, my father once said. I missed them, my parents.

IN MY CLASSROOM, portraits of the kings of Belgium hung on the wall above the blackboard, in frames with thick domed glass. Leopold II in the middle, just below Jesus Christ, was gazing out over the heads of the boys with the stern and righteous eyes of a king. The portrait bothered me. He had been the one who'd had the hands and feet chopped off Congolese children if they didn't tap enough rubber. Persistent rumours of bloodthirstiness and greed clung to his person like cobwebs. The newspapers were full of them. The more I looked at him—the sharp nose, the frizzled grey beard—the more convinced I was that the man was a murderer.

It was on a Friday afternoon, as the boys were doing their handwriting exercises and I was idly strolling through the class looking at the portrait, that the idea struck me to dethrone Leopold II in this classroom—even if he was no longer actually king and the only witnesses were nine of his former subjects. I decided to do it in a way the children would be able to relate to: smashing the glass of the frame by throwing marbles at it. I ended the handwriting lesson with the request that the boys should each bring two marbles—clay or glass—on Monday because we'd need them at the end of Flemish history lesson.

'Why two?' Etienne asked.

'Because everyone deserves a second chance,' I said.

The next Monday, at the end of the history lesson in which I had talked at length about the Congo Free State and Leopold II's role in it, I explained that a monarch should set a good example to his subjects. And that Leopold II had clearly failed to do that. They understood me perfectly, the cruel and bloody images I had fed them earlier still fresh in their minds: the scene of a father sitting on the ground with knees drawn up, staring at the lopped-off hand and foot of his five-year-old daughter who had not tapped enough rubber (I had seen an actual photograph of this, which of course I had not shown to them for pedagogical reasons), the image of the shed in which the severed hands and feet of the slaves were smoked for preservation, to be exchanged for a premium. Whipping, rape, kidnapping and mass murder. The boys were eyeing the portrait with withering stares, perfectly primed for what I had in mind. I walked to the back of the classroom and drew a circle on the floor with chalk.

'Each of you will take it in turn to throw your first marble at the portrait of Leopold II. I will call the winner by the name "Emperor of Goodness" for a week!'

The prize didn't appeal to them.

'And give him one franc!'

They cheered. Stamped their feet. Beat their chests like gorillas. I told them to concentrate and take careful aim, as they would only get two throws.

'Because everyone deserves a second chance,' Etienne shouted.

'That is an absolute moral imperative. A human being should not be judged by the worst fifteen minutes of his life,' I said, knowing full well that second chances were a rare thing in real life—though of course I didn't say so.

They looked at me impatiently, then I noticed Marcus had not moved from his desk. I went up to him.

'I don't want to throw anything at the king of Belgium,' he said softly when I was standing next to him.

'He's not the king anymore,' I said. 'Fortunately, the monarch we have now is a much juster man.'

'It feels wrong all the same.' He swallowed, and stared straight ahead. I asked him whether he minded someone else throwing for him. He didn't want that, either. Behind my back, the boys started cursing and swearing. I turned round and told them I would call off the game if I heard one more dirty word within these walls.

'He was not a good king,' I said. 'You heard as much today.'

'But doesn't he deserve a second chance too?'

'Very occasionally, people make such a complete mess of their first chance that they forfeit the second one,' I said to Marcus. I was starting to feel bad about the whole thing.

'That's what you say.'

'That's what I say.'

Jef was the first, and missed. He'd thrown with so much force, a piece of plaster flew off the wall. The marble clattered down on my desk and onto the floor tiles. The other boys roared, lousy shot! Chump! Get out of the circle and let Etienne have a go! Etienne nervously entered the circle, but just as he wanted to throw after taking aim with his right eye squeezed shut for a full minute, someone pushed him. The marble missed my vase with the arum lily by a whisker. He quickly stepped out of the circle and went to the back of the queue. Maurice Muylle did a little better. But only the twins' turns finally brought the desired result. Cyril's marble hit the edge of the portrait. It didn't even scratch the frame. Emiel hit the middle of the bubble. The glass was stronger than I had expected, though closer inspection revealed a crack.

Once everyone had had their first turn, we started again.

I was beginning to think the portrait of King Leopold II would stay in its place unscathed, that the eyes of this royal criminal would carry on burning into my back. To prevent this, I decided to give the boys a choice of missile from the geometric models we used in maths lessons: a cuboid, a pyramid, a sphere, a cone and a cylinder. Marcus was still sitting stiffly at his desk, his hands folded in his lap. Roger was the first to grab the sphere, which was wrested from his hands by Maurice, who in turn was elbowed in the face and started bawling. When I had restored order yet again, I positioned them with their backs against the cupboard, pacing to and fro in front of them like a disgruntled sergeant. I picked up the ball that had fallen to the floor and handed it to Roger. Back to the circle for the second round. It was a series of blunders. Not a single one of them hit the mark. When it was over, they stood there looking crestfallen, expecting me to stretch the rules of the game. I had no intention of doing that. Rules are rules, I said. You never, ever get a third chance. Forget it. There was nothing else for it, I would have to do it myself. But the moment I stepped into the circle, Marcus rose to his feet and announced with determination that he'd changed his mind and would give it a try after all. He took the ball out of my hands, stood in the circle and flung it into the middle of the portrait in a perfect arc. And at the exact moment that the portrait crashed down onto the tiles behind my desk, Father Storme entered the class-room.

In the early hours of Tuesday morning, I woke with a start. The boiling rage in the eyes of the priest when he saw the portrait of King Leopold II lying among the broken glass on the floor. His pent-up breath, his flushed face. My nightgown was sticky with sweat. The smell of mould was back, too. He had called the classroom a snake pit. Had frightened the boys with hell and damnation. He had made himself out to be the shepherd of the Elverdingen souls, the defender of the royal family, who took such pains to convert Negroes in Africa. I could see the doubt creeping into the boys' eyes as they flitted to and fro between the priest and me. I wouldn't put up with it. Not in my classroom. Not in front of my boys. I went up to him calmly, until I was close enough to touch him. The door was open, and with an outstretched arm, I emphatically demanded that he leave.

WE WENT BACK. A strong wind swept through the woods. There was something surreal about the contrast between the leafless, swaying branches of the tree tops and the mainly evergreen undergrowth, as if the wood had been turned upside down and the bare branches of the trees were their roots. I had thought about Myrtha a lot. The shot with which she had so unflinchingly dispatched Zaebos still reverberated through my mind.

She was splitting a log, in a dress with a deep slit up the side and a belt around her waist. When she lifted the axe, her thigh was exposed. She split the log and tossed the pieces on a pile behind her back. Then she looked in our direction and waved. Cali and Scox hadn't picked up our scent yet, but responded to her body language. They ran around her in a frenzy, romped together, froze for a few moments with pricked ears when they heard Ratface's call. Then they darted through a hole in the fence and bounded up the narrow path toward us. The memory of Zaebos's attack must undoubtedly have flashed through Ratface's mind, too, but the dogs only licked our extended hands, shoved their noses into our crotches. I was still looking at Myrtha, who leaned the axe against the chopping block, straightened her dress and walked toward us. Seeing her approach made me forget Ratface, the dogs, and even the wind whistling in my ears. Every sound was muffled, distant, a faint accompaniment to the image of Myrtha that attracted my eyes with an irresistible power. The realisation made my heart miss a beat. Then came the shame. Was I in love with a woman my mother's age? She stopped at the gate. Cali and Scox suddenly stuck their noses into the air, followed a trail to a spot on the grassy bank of the ditch. They wallowed in it, taking turns to rub their backs in the fresh carcass. She laid her hand on Ratface's shoulder. I followed them into the kitchen. Ratface didn't want to go inside. He wanted to run around with the dogs first. She showed him where to find the ball.

'Come in,' she said to me.

I sat at the table, feeling a trickle of sweat run from my armpit down the side of my body. And another one. She stood up and took my arm without a word, rolled up the sleeves of my shirt and examined my scars. The palm of her hand supporting my arm felt pleasantly warm, almost protective. Her other hand gently stroked the bumps and pits on my scalded skin. I was ashamed of that arm, and covered it up as much as possible. She kept running her fingers over it. I was wondering whether it was some kind of African ritual, but didn't pull away. The pain had long gone. The shame hadn't.

'Like a beautiful painting,' she said at last.

I doubted it.

'It's almost the shape of a tree.'

She traced the outline of a tree with her fingers. Her fingernail gleamed faintly.

'A tree whose crown is in full bloom.'

To my surprise, I started seeing it too: leaves and branches in the smooth patches of unevenly puckered skin, the rough relief of bark in the wrinkles underneath.

'The tree of knowledge of good and evil,' she said with a smile.

'Yggdrasil,' I said, to impress her.

'A Canadian poplar, more likely,' Ratface said behind us. I started. I hadn't heard him come in.

'Thin trunk,' he added.

I pulled my arm away.

'You said there'd be a surprise,' he said brashly. 'Last time we were here.'

'I know,' Myrtha said. 'Have an apple first.'

Once Ratface had obediently consumed his apple and placed the core on the table in front of him, she stood up. The three of us walked down the hall adjoining the kitchen. We stopped in front of a door. She paused for a moment, her hand already on the handle, and turned to us, giving Ratface a mysterious—and amused—look. He could hardly contain himself, and would have burst through the door if she hadn't been standing in front of it. The sudden flood of light hurt my eyes—the sun must have broken through the thick blanket of clouds. The room was lit like an imperial palace, scattered with rays of sunshine reflected by countless shiny objects. When my eyes had grown accustomed to the light, I saw it was an arsenal of weapons: spear points, knives, machetes, and pistols. Even a machine pistol. But that was not what Myrtha had meant to show Ratface, though he was already impressed. Our bodies cut through the dazzle of reflected rays. When we stood still, I could feel the heat of the sunlight my body was blocking.

She stopped at a massive door and pushed it open. A faint light. Nothing glittered. She pointed. Ratface whistled through his teeth. He had stopped in the doorway, and I pushed him forward gently. There, in the middle of the small, stuffy room, stood a male lion. Mouth open wide, as if it was yawning. Ratface ran up to it, stroked its mane and let his hand glide from the head over its back, all the way down to its buttocks. Then he went backward, rubbed his hand up against the fur, over bumps and scars, and ended by feeling the canines with his fingers. None of us had said a word yet. Even stuffed, the king of beasts commanded respect and fear.

'This was no ordinary lion,' Myrtha said. Her voice resonated in the small room.

'He was a man-eater.'

Ratface had understood her perfectly, but wanted to hear the word again.

'A man-eater,' she repeated.

'A lion that has tasted human flesh and wants to eat nothing else.'

Ratface looked into the open mouth, even put his hand in to feel the ribbed hard palate with his fingers.

'He killed fifteen soldiers before Leon was able to catch him.'

Leon Burns. The legendary warrior and decorated soldier. I already knew that. We had walked past his display of war medals and decorations.

'He and Zaebos.'

She put her finger on an almost invisible spot between the eyes. If you looked closely, you could see a whitish dent where the bullet had entered.

'A single bullet?'

Ratface continued his examination, seemingly without listening to her story. She hadn't been there, but had heard the long-drawn-out roar in her tent in the African night. A mortal fear had overcome her, then the shot rang out, and everything went silent. A different, awed silence, as if all the other animals knew what the roar meant. It was the only hunting trophy he ever had mounted. It cost a fortune to do, and another one to ship the thing all the way over here. But it had to be done. She stared at it intently.

'He was no angel.'

I didn't know whether she meant Leon or the beast. Then she walked out of the room. I followed her, banging my head against the concrete lintel above the door. Ratface stayed behind.

'His medals.' She pointed at the display case. The dazzle had gone. I spotted the machine pistol again. The beautifully grained wood of the butt. Short barrel.

'His favourite weapon. Never jammed.'

It didn't have a scratch. Not a spot of rust. He must have oiled and cleaned it constantly. The weapon attracted me. I wanted to hold it. She opened the glass door, took it out and handed it to me. It was curiously light. It was as if a blaze, a pilot light unexpectedly kindled by a gale, was scorching my insides. She saw it, snatched the gun from my hands and put it back. The spell was broken. There was a pile of boxes in a corner. Ammunition? Ratface came back. He wasn't interested in the objects and weapons in the cabinets any more. He wanted to go outside. To Cali and Scox. I stayed where I was, staring at the gun. She nudged me gently. Back in the kitchen, she poured coffee. The look in her eyes had changed; or perhaps it was the look in my eyes, as she dropped hers to the floor. She fiddled with the fabric of her dress, slowly running it through her fingers.

'Thanks for the surprise,' I said. 'Ratface really enjoyed seeing the lion. He'll always remember it.'

'So will you.'

'So will I,' I admitted.

'I have lots of them,' she said.

'What?'

'Memories. Experiences so intense they stick in your memory for ever.'

'I don't.'

'You're still young. It's up to you,' she said. 'You won't forget meeting Zaebos ever again, for instance. Life can suddenly take a turn, just like that. One of those unexpected twists of fate. You fear them, but you know there's no escaping them.'

I had no idea what she meant, but nodded anyway. She was looking at the photograph above my head.

'That's what happened to me,' she said, 'when I met Leon. It was love at first sight. He was a violent man, but never harmed me. He gave me years full of adventure. I'm grateful to him for that.'

But Leon was dead, and she was stuck here on her own, in a house on the edge of the woods, surrounded by useless weapons and medals and a stuffed lion.

'How did he die?'

'He committed suicide. With the gun you held in your hands earlier.'

She refilled my cup. I never drank coffee at home. I didn't like the taste, the colour was too black. Here, it tasted different.

The ball smashed through kitchen window. Shards of glass flew through the air, rattling down on and under the table. Into the coffee. Even on her black hair. Ratface came in. He apologized politely. He had thrown the ball with too much force, and it had slipped out of his hand. I was grateful to him. I stood up, bent over her head and picked the pieces of glass out of her hair. She let me. I could smell her, see the scalp at the parting of her hair, touched it with my fingertips. Excited, I went on searching for shards long after I had found the last one. She, meanwhile, calmed down Ratface, convinced him it would be all right, that she'd have a new pane put in, and asked him to tip our coffee down the sink. Lifting both arms, she combed her hair with her fingers and tied it back in a ponytail. For a moment, I could peer down into the depth between her shoulder blades. Skin as smooth and flawless as soap. Feeling the bulge in my trousers, I sat down quickly.

'Thank you,' she said.

'Another memory,' I said.

THERE HE STOOD. Victor Vanheule. And he'd seen me. I hadn't crossed the street this time but was walking on the pavement on the side of the pub. A man came outside. That voice. That boorish roar, cutting through the evening air. I slowed down, hoping to avoid meeting him. But he stopped to talk with Victor. I couldn't turn back, and it was too late to cross the road unnoticed. Farmer Verschoppen caught sight of me. The two of them awaited my approach in silence. Blocking my path, he asked me in a slurred voice why his son had had to smash the portrait of King Leopold II. For a moment, I felt Marcus had betrayed me.

'Good evening,' I said.

Victor nodded.

There was no point denying it, but I wanted to change the modality of his sentence.

'Since no one was obliged, he didn't have to do anything.'

My tone of voice disgusted me, it sounded almost apologetic.

'But he did it anyway,' Verschoppen said.

'Best shot of the class,' I said.

'Good for something, at least,' he mumbled.

'Have a nice evening,' I said. He planted his hand flat on my chest. The impact made me take a step backward. Victor didn't move.

'I haven't finished,' Verschoppen drawled.

He pushed his large hand against my chest with more force, as if wanting to lean on me, a tree he could take a good piss at.

'I am an officer in the Belgian army,' he said, squaring his shoulders and glowing with pride as he swayed in front of me. I could feel his tepid hand through my shirt. He said it without aggression. I didn't answer. Then he dropped his hand and took another step toward me. I could smell him.

'You shouldn't do things like that with the boys,' he said menacingly. Victor cautiously inched closer. I waited for Verschoppen's fist. A punch in the stomach. But I didn't move—I even felt a kind of inner calm, a sense of detachment. Verschoppen breathed heavily. Licked his lips several times. Then he seemed to realize we were not alone. Turning to Victor, he said, 'So my Marcus is a good shot, eh?'

'The best,' Victor said. He winked at me as he took Verschoppen by the arm and guided him back inside with gentle force.

My living room was as quiet as a graveyard. I lit a couple of candles and sat down. Just as I was getting comfortable, there was a knock at the door. There she stood, moonlight illuminating the back of her head. I was surprised. I couldn't imagine what she had come for. Marcus was doing fine. He was still top of the class. Was this about the matter of pelting the royal portrait with marbles? She let herself in, while my hand seemed to have fused with the handle, and opened the top buttons of her coat. Her necklace caught my eye, it glittered and flickered in the candlelight.

'I'm sorry to disturb you at this time of night,' she said.

'Not at all, Mrs Verschoppen,' I said.

She didn't want a cup of coffee. Or tea. I fetched the kitchen chair and sat down at the other end of the table.

Her face reminded me of a pen drawing I had once seen in one of my father's books.

'You're probably surprised to see me,' she said apologetically. 'But Marcus tells me so much about you. Only good things, believe me. He has become very fond of you.'

His small betrayal was still fresh in my mind, but her words warmed my heart all the same.

'I'm very fond of Marcus, too.'

'He talks about you every day; I feel I know you better than I actually do.'

That voice, full of emotion. That elegant poise. The way she laced her fingers in her lap. Just as I was about to interrupt the silence with some inane question, she went on.

'Of course I've also heard that he was the one who smashed the portrait of King Leopold II.'

'Well...'

'But I don't mind that at all. He told me he wouldn't do it at first, but that he joined in later. And it's true, that king *was* a greedy egoist.'

Silence.

'But that's not why I came. I've come to warn you. Father Storme can't stand the fact that you don't go to Mass. And he also says the things you do with and teach the boys are from the devil.'

A sudden flicker of the candle flame made her eyes shine. I saw the fine lines in the corners of her eyes, running into the tight skin of her temples like distributaries in a river delta.

'He really is furious,' she said.

Her voice and words were perfectly matched to the dusky gloom of my room.

'Religious belief is a personal matter.'

'I agree with you entirely. But this is a village. And besides, you go beyond the personal yourself by telling the boys there is no heaven or hell.'

I tried to guess her age. She had to be in her late thirties or early forties. Marcus was twelve. If she had married fairly late, it would be about accurate. She put her hands on the table, fingers still woven together.

'You are young. As I understand it, this is your first job. Surely you don't want to lose it?'

'Because of Father Storme?'

'He has friends in high places.'

Her voice trailed off.

'I had to tell you.'

She buttoned up her coat. I thanked her, sorry to see her leave. Not a word about her husband's antipathy toward me. Maybe she wasn't aware of it. I heard her heels clicking over the cobbles. Then she suddenly turned and hurried back.

'I almost forgot, I haven't been able to thank you for helping Marcus that time at the coal seller's,' she said.

I waved it aside. She went to the bicycle she had leaned against the fence, and rode away. I stood in the doorway for a long time. The moon appeared from behind a slowly drifting cloud. No stars glittered in the sky.

The seat of her chair was still warm. I put my hand on it, covering her warmth with mine. I sniffed it, smelled the fabric, the backrest. A slight hint of lavender. I knew the scent well from Mother's herb garden when I was a boy. To stem the tide of thoughts and emotions flooding me, I stood up and went outside. Spiney was in his usual place underneath the board. After a short chat, I wished him a good night. Then I climbed the stairs, undressed and crept into the trough.

NEXT MORNING IN the classroom: 'Sir! Sir! Roger keeps farting!' Maurice said, holding his nose.

'Come on, Roger, pinch your hole shut!' Walter shouted.

'I don't know what you mean,' Rogers said.

'That's even worse,' Jef said.

'He reeks like a muck spreader!' Etienne said.

'Next time we take him prisoner him on Saturday, I'll put his balls in a vice,' Maurice chuckled, tugging at his braces. Roger blushed. I saved him from any more humiliating remarks by calling Maurice and Etienne to the front. Gingerly, they climbed onto the stone platform where I waited for them with a ruler in my left hand and a long stick of chalk in my right. Maurice thrust his hands in his trouser pockets and Etienne twiddled his thumbs nervously. Both of them looked up, eyes searching my face for a clue to what would come next. Keeping them in suspense just a little longer, I looked over their crowns at the other boys. Then I put the chalk and ruler down on my desk, picked up the bag leaning against it and took out a bundle of rags. At least, that's what Maurice and Etienne must have thought as they watched me painstakingly laying out the crumpled pieces of fabric on my desk. Once I had given them a shake and displayed them in front of the boys, they could tell they were costumes. Etienne scratched behind his ears and Maurice hitched up his trousers, exchanging glances—they smelled a rat.

'Here, put this on,' I said, handing them the clothes.

The others burst out laughing, Roger the loudest, in his shrillest, nastiest voice.

'Suits Etienne's pointy ears perfectly!' he shrieked.

I turned round and ordered Roger to come forward too. He stayed seated, staring back at me defiantly, but eventually gave in and came to the front. I reached into the drawer and took out a long cardboard tongue, which I had drawn, cut out and coloured the day before. I had threaded a length of string through it and now hung the tongue around Roger's neck. I also pulled a cap with two donkey's ears over his head.

'Roger will be the thirsty donkey,' I told the rest of the boys, who didn't have the courage to start laughing again. I knew from the terrified delight shining in their eyes that I had their full attention. Maurice was sulking, and refused to put on the costume. I wasn't about to let him off the hook, however; not if I'd have to pull the clothes over his hide personally. Etienne was already wearing his snow-white robe. The wires in the wings on his back rasped against the blackboard. I gave him a bow and arrow I had made myself. He was thrilled. Maurice had finally managed to put on his black costume. I shoved a whip into his hands, braided from shoots of the old pollard willow by the mud hills. He immediately started swishing it dangerously. I waited patiently until they had let off steam, then ordered them to stand in a row, the thirsty donkey in the middle. I demanded silence before posing my question.

'Boys, what does this look like to you?'

'Fancy dress,' Jef said.

'A circus,' Walter corrected.

'A donkey that is so thirsty it is having a fever dream?' Cyril asked.

'An angel and a devil,' someone shouted.

'And what about me?' Roger asked me.

I shrugged my shoulders.

'Am I an ill donkey?' he asked.

'No.'

'Then why is my tongue hanging out like that?'

'Because you're hungry and thirsty. You have sweated and toiled the whole day, and now you're tired,' Marcus said.

I could live with that. Roger gave the tongue around his neck another tug and squinted at his classmates.

'Well, boys, what else do you think this scene represents?' I asked again.

'The donkey is the angels' slave,' Jef said.

'Animals are always slaves,' Emiel said.

'But don't you have to be human to be a slave?' Walter asked, looking at me.

'On a pirate ship, for instance,' Cyril said.

'And if you don't row fast enough, you're hanged or keelhauled,' Emiel said.

It wasn't where I wanted this to go, so I said,

'Etienne, give the donkey something to drink.' Etienne cupped his hands and held them out to Roger, who pretended to slurp up the water.

'Maurice, pretend you are whipping the donkey.'

Maurice perked up at this and pretended to give Roger's back a furious thrashing, while Roger acted his part brilliantly by flinching at each blow.

'The white figure is good and the black one's bad,' Walter said.

It was a start.

'But they are both the donkey's masters,' Jef said.

'Only one of them can be the master,' Cyril said.

'So here we have good and bad,' I said, giving Walter an

approving look. 'Now watch this.'

I told black Maurice to feed the donkey and Etienne to shoot an arrow at Roger with his bow, who, in another skilfully acted scene, pretended to pull it out of his hole with a grimace.

'They are both good and bad,' Walter said, visibly confused.

'We're all donkeys,' Marcus said.

'Go on.'

'And we meet good and bad people in our lives.'

'But you never know which ones are good and which are bad,' Cyril said.

'You can only tell by the things they say or do,' Marcus said.

'But someone who does a good thing, can do something bad, too,' Jef said.

They were beginning to understand.

I told Roger to put his arms around Etienne and Maurice and smile at both of them lovingly.

'If someone shot an arrow into my bum or gave me a whipping, I'd want to get even with them,' Emiel said.

'So would I,' Jef said.

'You should never take it lying down, my father always says,' Roger said.

'No, never,' they all agreed.

'All of you sometimes hurt the donkey, and sometimes you're kind to it,' I said. 'If you take someone prisoner by the mud hills on Saturday and torture him, you hurt that boy. But the next Monday, you're back here playing together on the playground, best of friends.'

'So that means we can be both black and white,' Marcus said.

'Yes,' I said. 'But you can always choose which you want to be most.'

'I think black's the nicer colour,' Roger said.

'Me too,' Jef said, 'and if we're black and hurt someone, we can just go to confession. Then we're white again and our sins are gone.'

'It's not that simple,' I said sternly. I would like to have kept the Catholic faith out of this, but couldn't ignore his remark.

'How so?'

'Deep down, you know—you feel—whether what you do is good or bad. Only if you choose to do bad things do you need to go to confession afterward. Exactly because Father Storme has made you believe that confession takes away all your sins, you have the courage to do bad things.'

'So we're not allowed to play at torture anymore on Saturdays?' Roger sounded disappointed.

'Make sure you don't hurt each other too much.'

They beat their chests and grinned at each other.

I wanted to say something more about confession, but bit my tongue.

And then came the question. Out of the blue. I didn't even know who asked it.

'Sir! Sir! What's your favourite weapon?'

There I stood, after giving an explanation about good and bad in humans, confronted with the question of my favourite weapon.

'I ... I don't have one,' was all I managed to stammer. I could feel the smooth wood in my hands again. The remarkable lightness. The deep glow. The disenchantment when Myrtha took the machine pistol out of my hands and placed it back in the display cabinet.

'But if you actually had to go to war, what weapon would you choose?' Jef asked.

'I think the weapon chooses you,' I told the class.

I HEARD A noise outside the door. Godaleva's face flashed through my mind, but so did farmer Verschoppen's mug, and even the wrathful features of Father Storme. Curious, I pushed back my chair and went to the door. A quick peek through the window first. It was the postman. I readily accepted his explanation for the letter being late—it had fallen behind the pile and not turned up until yesterday—and his apologies for disturbing me on a Saturday morning. I told him not to worry. He was well aware I never received any post. I could tell at a glance who the letter was from. The militant 't's rising above the ranks like war banners, the consistently forward-slanting letters like footsoldiers pushing against the wind on the ruled lines of the page. It was a letter from my father. Only a note, really, in which he politely asked after my well-being. Whether I was able to handle a class of eight farmer's boys. And whether I had a seat on the village council yet, as the teacher of Year Six is bound to command some authority in such a village. The day I left home, I vowed not to get in touch with my parents until they did. I knew in my heart that my father had forgiven me for what had happened. Not a word from Mother. Judging by the post mark, the letter was a month old already. I folded it up and placed it in the middle of the table.

IT WAS THE last Friday before the Christmas holidays. I stayed on after school for the report card meetings. The boys' best drawings adorned the blackboard behind my back.

When the church bells struck six o'clock, I sat down regally at my desk. I'd made sure the classroom was tidy and had even polished the top of my desk by rubbing its surface with a wet cloth. The dents I had knocked into the desk with my ruler were covered with school books, and I was quietly pleased with the metamorphosis of the cloudy chalk marks on the blackboard into a pitch-black, glossy surface. Within a minute, I heard heels clicking over the playground, and a plump woman with short legs slowly opened the door. She had curly hair. I stood up, greeted her with a majestic air from behind my desk and motioned her to sit down on one of the chairs in front of me. She timidly walked to the front and sat down.

'You are Etienne Veugelaere's mother?'

A nod. She seemed extremely tense, bowing her head so low that I was presented with a tangled crown.

'Good … well, I am glad to say Etienne has made some progress, compared to last year's report. His performance has improved by'—I cast a quick glance at the report card lying in front of me—'four per cent. He really does his best in all subjects, even though he finds it difficult at times.'

What I was saying about her son seemed to come as a relief to her, she met my eyes for a moment but dropped hers again an instant later. Wanting to reassure her, I rambled on about her son's commitment, his unflagging interest in most subjects and his helpfulness. To my amazement, I even heard myself say that he was one of the leaders of the class, a statement that was completely untrue, as Etienne followed the others like a sheep. I put this fabrication down to nerves. I mentioned neither the lamentable progress he had made in physics, nor the fact he was unable to remember even the simplest multiplication table. When I stopped talking to give her the opportunity to say something, or perhaps ask a question, she didn't react, but continued to stare at the wooden front panel of my desk. Did I look so strict and unapproachable she didn't even have the courage to face me? I had run out of things to say. When the silence became too awkward, she mustered all her courage and looked up. She thanked me. I could hardly understand her. Then I saw the reason for her silence and embarrassment: she had an enormous overbite. I had to make a great effort not to look at it. She stood up, mumbling another thank you and disappeared faster than she had come. My throat felt gritty, as if I had swallowed a sandy piece of bread.

Luckily, the next two meetings went more smoothly.

Then Marcus's parents came in. Farmer Verschoppen leading the way in a pinstripe suit. Hair cropped short. For the first time, I noticed the size of his hands. I stood up straight again to welcome them from behind the desk. Godaleva followed. She was wearing a black skirt and high black boots. A white woollen sweater appeared as she took off her jacket and draped it neatly over the back of the chair. Farmer Verschoppen waited a few moments before sitting down, and Mr Vantomme's advice went through my mind: I should try not to get into his bad books. He sat down, took off his jacket and rolled up his shirt sleeves. Then he crossed his arms over his chest. He started talking before I had a chance to open the conversation.

'Is Marcus able to hold his own against the other lads?'

I wasn't so much surprised at the question as annoyed at not having the first word, and felt no obligation to answer him. Instead, I started talking about Marcus's excellent report card as planned.

'Your son is top of the class. He excels in all subjects.'

I liked the smile around her lips, though I couldn't tell whether she was smiling at my praise of her son or my defying her husband. Outside, a gust of wind swept over the playground. Verschoppen was more interested in the question of Marcus holding his own than his results, and asked again. I looked at him for the first time, my eyes having travelled to and fro between Marcus's report card on my desk, the window that was still cracked and Godaleva's face until now.

'Marcus is perfectly capable of looking after himself among the other boys.'

That contented smile on her face again.

'Does he get into fights?' he asked.

'Fights?'

The word nettled me.

'But Mr Verschoppen, that is not allowed. At school, the boys are to behave themselves at all times.'

The image of Roger with his balls in a noose flashed through my mind. The corners of Verschoppen's mouth twisted downward. He pushed his chin out.

'As I have said, your son shines in all subjects. You have every right to be proud of such a child.'

'Mr Verbocht, you must have noticed that Marcus can be a bit feeble at times. We'—Godaleva shot him a sideways glance at this point—'find it very important that he gets enough physical exercise, and plays with the other boys. He needs toughening up. But all he's interested in is drawing and reading,' he said, with a significant look at the butterfly drawing behind my back.

'Those are the kind of skills that make us human,' I said.

She carefully brushed a stray wisp of hair behind her ear.

'He is my only son. He will inherit the farm, be in charge of the farmhands, introduce new farming innovations like nitrogen-based artificial fertiliser and the dynamo, which is used more and more in machines. But he's not interested in technology, either. And when I take him all over the country to visit fairs, he crawls off into a corner to draw.'

The mere thought of it made him choke.

'I'm glad you have seen the light as regards the dynamo, and that we may be saved the unpleasant smell of real manure in the future; but your son's interests lie elsewhere. And there isn't a power on Earth that can change that, unless of course you want to make him miserable by forcing him.'

'How dare you claim I want to make my own son miserable?'

A quick glance at the face of Marcus's mother told me she was still enjoying my polite and controlled defiance. I went on. 'Marcus is a highly intelligent, sensitive boy who must be given the opportunity to develop his gifts and talents.'

'Marcus is going to work with me on the farm, starting next year. There will be no more time for school,' Verschoppen said.

He sprang to his feet and marched out of the classroom. Without her.

Godaleva stood up and extended her hand. She apologized for her husband's behaviour. It was a sensitive topic.

He was not a bad man, not at all, she said, just down-to-earth and stubborn. She was very glad to hear Marcus was doing well. She agreed his drawings were beautiful.

I had stood up and walked to the other side of my desk without realizing it. Her eyes were full of gratitude, but I also sensed the resilience of her personality. She had not followed her husband when he stood up and left. It hadn't rattled her in the least.

'Marcus really must continue his education,' I said decisively. 'I do hope your husband didn't mean what he said about keeping him at home next year.'

'He does mean it,' she said. 'But the last word has not been said.'

I felt the same sense of security I had experienced visiting her house. This was a strong woman. A rock that couldn't be crushed. And attractive. I sat down again quickly, a sudden weakness in my legs making me unsteady. She left the classroom, looking at me over her shoulder before going through the door.

RESISTING THE TEMPTATION of Bollemeer Lane, I turned away from the church. Victor was at his post, next to the slot window of the Pumphouse. A ray of light slipping out of the narrow opening surrounded his head like a crown. I felt like going over for a chat, but a voice inside me said that it wouldn't be wise, that the many silences, the many half-expressed thoughts would only disrupt our remote friendship. He was not much of a talker anyway. So I simply returned his nod amicably and walked on.

The scents in Forest Lane did not disappoint me. They were strongest shortly before sunset, as if making one last effort before nightfall, knowing they would be slowly drowned by the morning dew. There was a bright moon with a wisp of grey, unravelled cloud behind it like the tail of a comet. It looked like a painting. I was studying the sky so intently I almost tripped over a cobblestone sticking out above the others. Cursing, I looked up at the strange spectacle again, but the comet's tail had drifted away and the moon stood out even more against the dark blue. Walking further down the lane, I kept my eyes on the brightly lit window of the castle in the distance. I imagined the speck of light was the end of a tunnel, a pinprick of sunshine, and that I was a half-blind mole digging furiously in the pitch dark with my paws to get away from the other moles, who were hunting me for my velvety white coat.

Before I was halfway through the lane, I was sure I had seen a shadow flit past the light from the window. A bat, perhaps. Or an owl. It had happened in an instant, but I was sure I had seen it. I stood still, staring intently at the light. Just as I was about to go on, the light disappeared again for a fraction of a second. Standing in the middle of the lane, I suddenly felt uneasy. I thought about turning back, to the safest corner of Elverdinge, where Victor was standing watch. But my sense of honour prevented me. Had I just heard a snapping twig? My hands left the warm hollows of my trouser pockets. The yellow light from the castle suddenly resembled the forbidding eye of a Cyclops. I pulled myself together. Perhaps it had been the village constable, cruising over Vlamertinge Street on his bike. And then turning back because he had dropped his lighter, as he had wanted to light a cigarette while cycling. But then he would have to ride past a third time. Making an effort to suppress any morbid thoughts, I glanced over my shoulder and walked on quickly.

I hadn't gone thirty paces when I heard the sound of voices in the undergrowth. Voices trying not to be heard. Then a muffled curse. I pricked up my ears. They were giving away their position without realizing it. I felt a sudden confidence. I was the one spying on them, they had no idea they were being overheard and followed. I quickly stepped into the grass between the twin row of poplars, supple and hunched forward like a hunter, and crept another dozen metres toward the voices. Once I was able to understand what they said, I squatted down in front of a thick trunk, leaning my shoulder against the bark. Twigs cracked as they moved. They went deeper into the woods. I followed. Then they stopped. I squatted behind another tree. There was a silence, and something that sounded like a struggle. Panting. The sharp jangle of the metal clasp of a belt, the sound of tearing fabric. I listened carefully. Maybe they had kidnapped some poor devil in a potato sack and were about to finish him off. Strangle him with a belt. Should I intervene? Play the hero? But why risk my life for someone I didn't know from Adam? Then I heard a voice say, 'Stick it in, c'mon kid, slowcoach, get on your knees. My bum's getting cold.'

Something fell to the ground. I expected a woman to speak, but the second voice was male too, deeper than the first.

'You little bully, I'm going to give you a good pounding!'

'Yes. Yes. You do that!'

'And then it's my turn, eh? Eh!? You hear me?'

'Shut up and get on with it!'

I'll never forget the revolting sounds that followed. The little bully's shrill voice also etched itself indelibly into my mind. It went on and on. Then more struggling. The click of another belt. A thump. More panting. I didn't feel like a hunter in a primeval forest anymore. I decided to leave. But as I turned, my foot caught in a hole in the ground. I lost my balance and fell. I didn't move for a few seconds, but I could tell from the panic in their voices that they'd heard me. Scrambling to my feet, I ran. I took a detour home so I'd be seen by as few people as possible, knowing full well it wouldn't be difficult to work out who was taking a walk in Forest Lane at that time of night.

CHRISTMAS HOLIDAYS 1913. The school was closed for a fortnight. It was hailing and the temperature was arctic. I kept the stove burning all day, and stirred up the fire when I woke at night from the cold. Every other day, I ran out of coal and had to fetch a fresh scuttleful. After I had walked through the freezing cold to haul my scuttle onto the scales a few times, the coal dealer told me he could come round with his cart and deliver a load to my house. All I'd have to do then was shovel it into the coal shed. The amount of money he charged for it was ridiculously high. Besides, I had neither a wheelbarrow nor a coal shed. The smile on his lips didn't reach his eyes when I reluctantly refused the offer.

I dreaded the prospect of spending the holidays alone. Godaleva haunted my mind. I had a fantasy about her preparing a feast for me, apron tied tightly around her waist, the bow of the ribbon nestled in the curve of her lower back, hair gathered in a bun. And her long, slender fingers, with no rings, carefully rinsing the lettuce, seasoning the meat. Marcus, relaxed in her presence. Until Verschoppen comes in, ignores his son and starts groping her with his large, dirty hands.

One morning between Christmas and New Year, my father unexpectedly turned up at my door. He came in, hung his jacket over the back of the chair and hugged me.

I was touched. After the embrace, he pushed himself away from me, gripping my shoulders with his hands.

'You look worn out, my boy,' he said.

He didn't look too well himself. His face was ashen, tufts of grey hair sticking out on all sides, clothes crumpled from the journey. But I caught a glimpse of the old glimmer in his eyes, a zest for life that danced around his pinprick pupils like a spark. They were more watery than I remembered them.

'Sit down,' I said, as I quickly fetched a chair for him from the kitchen, pushed it toward him and hurried back to fill the kettle for coffee. I smacked the kettle onto the stove with too much force, spilled water hissing and steaming on the hotplate. I sat down opposite him. We talked and talked—about the boys in my class; about village life; about his job—and only stopped to eat a quick sandwich. We carefully steered clear of the past, and of Mother, focusing our conversation on the present and a little bit of the future. We drank more coffee. White. He had brought me supplies: soap, a razor, eau de cologne, which he handed to me ceremoniously.

'How is Mother?' I asked.

Silence.

Then, 'She's better.'

'Does she get out of bed more often now? Does she tend her herb garden again?'

'The herb garden's gone,' he said. 'There's a kennel in its place now. She's taken in a stray dog.'

'That's good,' I said, surprised—I couldn't remember Mother ever wanting a dog.

'She talks to it a lot, to the dog,' he said. 'It even sleeps in our bedroom at night, in a basket on her side of the bed.'

I deduced from his words she had not forgiven me. Seeing my dismay, he said, 'The presents were her idea, by the way.'

I wanted to believe him.

'Thank her from me.'

He checked his watch. He had to go home. The last train left Ypres in less than an hour. We stood up and embraced a second time. Feeling my father's arms around me did me the world of good. He promised to come again. Long after he had left I could feel the warmth of his hand in mine.

IN THE FIRST school week of the new year, I noticed that Marcus's shoulders were slumped more than usual. Had he hurt himself? Had his father given him a thrashing?

'Sir! Sir! Why'd you never go to Mass on Sundays?'

Roger. Who else. He didn't give me time to answer before going on, 'Surely you're not too busy on Sundays, are you? You don't have no cows or a wife and children.'

'Very perceptive of you, Roger,' I said.

'Or perhaps you have a sweetheart somewhere?' Roger asked.

The question sounded more disrespectful than it was meant.

'Roger is an altar boy now,' Etienne said.

'A useless one,' Walter said. 'He only does it because Father Storme always gives him a tip.'

'Not true!' Roger cried, outraged.

I could tell from the way he was blinking that it was.

'So he can go drinking like his father,' Jef said jealously— his father wouldn't take him along to the pub yet.

'At least my father doesn't come crawling home,' Roger said. His voice had a nasty edge. I decided to intervene.

'Come, come, let's not use one another unkindly.'

'How so?'

'Whuk?'

'Let's be nice to each other. And no, Roger, I don't have a

sweetheart,' I added with a forced smile.

'Sir! Sir!' A highly unusual sight: Maurice Muylle had an urgent question. His arm straight up in the air, his index finger pointing up like the warning of an angry father. He was clearly not about to give up, even using his other arm to prop up the raised one. I nodded at him.

'Why not?' It took me a while to realize that his question referred to my last remark, not the particularly difficult part of the lesson I had been taking great pains to explain. I was standing on the front edge of the stone platform. My suit had become baggy of late. My forehead felt hot.

'Because that's just the way it is,' I answered curtly.

'But you're a teacher!'

'And what, pray, does that signify?'

'That you never have to get your hands dirty and always go to work in a smart white shirt.'

'That's true enough,' I said. 'But it has nothing to do with the question whether or not I should have a sweetheart.'

'But surely women notice you more than us farmers?'

Maurice was like a dog with a bone.

'I'd have to want to notice them too, Maurice,' I said, suddenly realizing I never did that: catch someone's gaze and hold it. Not even Godaleva's.

'Physics! Get out your exercise books!' I cleared my throat and went on quickly, 'Everyone take out their bags of leaves and their herbaria. I've asked you to collect leaves and press them in a book, or under some heavy weight, so they dry up nice and flat. Choose one leaf of each species, see if you can identify it and then glue it in the correct place in your herbarium.'

'But I forgot to bring my glue,' Etienne said.

'Me, too,' Cyril said.

A wave of hopelessness washed over me. My heart drowned in my rib cage. I had recently been torn between using a strict approach with the boys and engaging them in a calm, patient dialogue. And they had picked up the scent of my indecision like a pack of young bloodhounds, slowly but surely extending their territory.

'You can both use mine,' Marcus said, seeing my indecision. He held out the triangular blue glass jar in his outstretched hand.

'We don't want yours. It don't stick proper!' Cyril shouted.

'It's girls' glue!' Etienne shouted.

It was the dull pain in his eyes, the shoulders slumping even more and my powerlessness in the face of this cruel rejection of his offer that made me grab my ruler. I lashed out, hitting the desk first and then, with less force, the fingers I had ordered them to stretch out. Until my anger was spent. Then I walked back to my desk, disgusted with myself, their cries of pain still ringing in my ears. Every sob of the two weeping dunces burned into my heart with the heat of a fever. I felt dizzy. Marcus had watched me with frightened eyes. In the sudden brightness of the sunlit classroom, I wearily gave the boys permission to leave early. School was out for the day.

It was dark by the time I got home. I had spent my surplus salary on vegetables from the grocer's shop. I selected a shallot, chopped it into thin strips and tipped the pile into the hot butter spitting in a frying pan on the stove. The fat spattered my trousers. Mr Vantomme had given me another pile of newspapers. To distract myself and to forget that afternoon's incident, I read a short history of American convicts put to death in the electric chair. A pen drawing of a certain William Kemmler, the first man to be killed by means of electricity, lingered in my mind long after I had taken the paper outside to the privy. To make sure the chair worked, the scientists had electrocuted a horse the day before. The article described how a round patch of hair was shaved from Kemmler's scalp, and that they even cut a hole into his suit to stick a cable through. He fumed like a cigar, and some even claimed he burst into flames in his chair. But while blood vessels exploded underneath his skin, his heart stubbornly went on beating. The voltage was doubled. Apparently, even the most vindictive onlookers wanted to leave the room. The article closed with the heartrending conclusion that the gallows or axe might have been preferable. Folding the paper and staring into the stinging mist dispersed by the charred shallot, I couldn't shake off an ominous feeling that man was the basest of all the world's species.

That night, I dreamed I was sitting at the table. My mother was sitting opposite. Just the two of us. A greasy strand of hair fell forward from behind her ear as she bent over to butter my bread. As I watched, the strand changed into a snake. The serpent, that kept growing longer, wriggled across the tabletop, between the glasses and cups, the butter dish and jam jar, and opened its gigantic mouth in front of my eyes. Just as it was about to sink its venomous fangs into my skull, I awoke, screaming with fear.

AFTER WEEKS OF hard work, I decided to treat myself to a steak.

'And? How are you getting along with the boys of Year Six?' the butcher asked. He had his back turned to me, his small cleaver chopping through bone with a crunch that went through me like a knife.

'Fine.'

I didn't much feel like a chat because I was looking forward to getting back home as soon as possible, sitting close to the stove and tucking into the warm, bloody meat of my steak with a glass of beer.

'Any luck making them brighter, or is it a hopeless task?'

'Each child is different,' I answered.

My sentence was chopped in two by the thud of his cleaver on the block.

'If they're no good at schoolwork, they'll just have to learn a trade, same as me. Started working for my late father when I was twelve.'

At this he finally turned round, wiping his bloody hands on his apron. He had a sharp nose. His earlobes were large and red, reminding me of a cock's wattle. He bent over and took a juicy cut of meat from the pile. He slapped it onto the scales.

'Half a kilo exactly. Think you can manage that? 'Cos you don't look like someone who eats a lot.'

'I'll manage.'

'But then of course you can just walk it off again, eh?'

I laughed politely, paid and turned to go. Closing the door behind me, I spotted Godaleva cycling toward me in the distance. The mist of her breath like fleeting little clouds in her neck. I waited. She had seen me too, and was waving. Her white, thigh-high stockings emphasized the rounded muscles of her calf. Each movement of her legs had an air of modest decency as she cleaved through the street, bolt upright in the saddle. Vantomme was right. At every breeze that lifted her skirt, your eyes involuntarily searched the white flesh of her buttocks. She leapt off her bike a few metres away from me, cheeks flushed. A fox-fur stole around her neck. She leaned her bike against the brick wall and smoothed down her skirt.

'Good day, David.'

'Godaleva,' I said, suppressing the shiver tingling down my spine. The bag with the steak was bumping against my thigh. She took off her gloves.

'I enjoy cycling, even in this cold weather,' she said.

She hesitated. It was too cold to stand still for very long, but she didn't go into the butcher's shop.

'Mr Verbocht. I have a favour to ask. I was wondering whether you'd mind taking Marcus with you on your Sunday walks.'

The question caught me off guard. Fond as I was of Marcus, I wasn't keen on the idea of someone accompanying me on my walks. They were the moments I could stroll through the countryside in a daydream, without having to pay much attention to anything or anyone. But if I turned down her request, I would have wasted a chance of seeing more of her.

'He's constantly been catching colds lately and hardly goes outdoors anymore. It will do him so much good.' The consternation in her voice touched me. It was a dignified plea. She could tell I was wavering. I would have liked to ask whether farmer Verschoppen knew about this plan, and what he thought about it, when I realized the time had been carefully chosen. He would be boozing in the pub. I wondered whether that was deliberate.

'Of course I'll take him along,' I said reluctantly.

'You have no idea how happy that makes me,' she said. For the first time I saw her lips widen further than her usual pursed smile. Her teeth were straight, and all the more conspicuous for their temporary release from those lips. She made a step toward me, the smile still on her face. That smile, meant for me alone, in which she momentarily exposed a part of herself to me. For a moment I thought—hoped—that she would kiss me, or throw her arms around my neck.

'May I drop him off at your place tomorrow after Mass?'

'Tomorrow? Won't it be too cold for him to … ?'

'Having a change of heart already?' she teased.

'Tomorrow's fine,' I said.

She gave me a long look. Cursing my shyness, I cast down my eyes. Then she turned round and went into the shop. I crossed the road. It took all the willpower I could muster to keep my eyes straight ahead of me without looking back.

Sunday morning. There he was. In his Sunday best, hair glistening with brilliantine. I had watched them coming from the moment they turned the corner, Godaleva pushing her bike. She stopped at the gate, holding the handlebars, one foot on the pedal. When she caught sight of me she smiled and rode off, hopping on her free foot until she had gathered enough momentum to put it on the other pedal. Her skirt billowed and she pushed it down between her buttocks with her left hand. I was standing on the wrong side. For a time, I stared after her over Marcus's head, lost in thought. He coughed.

'Hello, Marcus,' I said, a little irritated that his cough had jolted me out of my blissful daydream. I asked him to come in. He was ill at ease.

'Would you like something to drink first?'

'No, thank you, sir.'

'No need to call me "sir". We're not at school now,' I said.

His face was pale. The delicate black eyebrows looked almost as though they had been pencilled onto it. He reminded me of the smartly-dressed mannequins and their artificial-looking faces I saw in the windows of the clothes shops in Ghent on the day I bought my suit.

'Come,' I said. 'I want you to meet someone.'

He followed me through the house to the back door.

'Small place,' he said as he pulled the door shut behind him and looked at my weed garden. I coaxed him over the trampled-down path. I knew Spiney would be there because I'd checked earlier.

'Let me introduce you to a friend of mine,' I said as we were both crouching down beside the board.

'His name's Spiney.' I stuck out my finger and Spiney sniffed at it.

'Wow, a tame hedgehog!' Marcus cried. He went down on his knees. I wanted to say something about his Sunday trousers, but it was too late anyway. Marcus held out his finger too, and lo and behold, Spiney didn't roll up in a ball. I took the jar of worms and snails I had collected that morning and gave it to Marcus. He selected the fattest one and dangled it in front of Spiney's pointy snout. Spiney grabbed the worm with his front paws and started munching it.

'Can't we stay here instead of going for a walk?' Marcus asked.

'No, I promised your mother we'd walk.'

'But sir, don't hedgehogs hibernate?'

'They usually do, yes,' I said; I had wondered about that myself.

'So why doesn't Spiney?'

'Probably because of the comfortable little den I've made for him and the abundant worms and snails I feed him.'

He stroked the spines.

'Come on, let's go,' I said.

On the church square, we saw a crowd of people standing next to one of the white stone pillars. I had noticed the pillars before, which surrounded the church like a fairy ring, but had never wondered what they meant. Father Storme, standing on some kind of elevation, towered over the surrounding crowd. He was right beside the pillar. His voice carried over to us. I recognized some of the people in the crowd, looking solemn in their dark grey or black suits and coats, but most of them were strangers to me. I must have muttered something to myself, as Marcus answered:

'It's the *Ommegang* procession.'

'Never heard of it,' I said, without embarrassment.

He looked at me in surprise.

'The white, upright blocks are the stations. There are six of them around the church, and the seventh is inside the church.'

'Interesting.'

'Once a year, the whole procession is done. The people stop to pray at each block.'

The thought of the crowd standing and mumbling at seven of those pillars amused me.

'If you went closer, you'd see the images carved on them. On the first one, Saint Livinus is ordained as archbishop. On the second, he's converting the Flemish. On the third he's distributing alms, on the fourth he's curing the sick, on the fifth his tongue is torn out and thrown to the dogs, and on the sixth he's beheaded ... '

'Not much left of Saint Livinus in the end, then,' I said lightly, though I was impressed by little Marcus's knowledge.

'But didn't you say there were seven?' I asked.

'Yes, yes. The seventh one is inside the church. A miraculous statue of the saint.'

'With his head and tongue back in their proper place, I assume?'

Marcus nodded.

'What an unusual spectacle,' I said, watching the crowd shuffle to the fifth station. The priest led the way, carrying a stool under his arm, half concealed by the black fabric of his sleeves. He placed the stool beside the next pillar, pressed its legs firmly into the ground and climbed on it.

'Dear parishioners! Let us pray for Saint Livinus, whose tongue, as you can see here, was ripped out by the unbelievers of the world, the heathens, who thought they could silence him that way. But great was their amazement when they saw what happened next!'

He paused, and staring over the heads of the crowd, noticed us. His mouth hung open for a few moments, but not a sound came out of his throat. Some heads in the front row turned to look at us. Recovering his voice, he spoke with even more passion than before.

'What happened then was God's mercy! The damnation of the unbelievers! Yes, they cut out his tongue, and yes, they threw it to the dogs. But lo! Look here! His tongue immediately grew back!'

He touched Saint Livinus's cheek with his index finger and tapped it several times.

'A miracle! A marvel! And when the unbelievers realized

they had been wrong, they showed remorse, screamed and begged forgiveness. But it was too late. God's mercy has limits. They were destroyed, drowned and burned. That is what must happen to heathens! And it shall!'

A mutter went through the crowd. I was not impressed, though I had to admit the priest was a master in the art of storytelling. When the parishioners had finished mumbling a series of prayers, he leapt from his stool and walked to station number six. There was even an old stray dog waddling after him. Marcus wanted to stay for the sixth story, but I nudged him gently and said we should be going. We walked along the front of the church, and past the black gate that only the altar boys were allowed to go through because there, hidden behind a gigantic shrub around the corner, was the door of the sacristy. Hundreds of graves surrounded the church, some with decorative tombstones carved of yellow limestone. Others had worm-eaten wooden crosses. We came past the main entrance and the graveyard gate next to it. To my surprise, there was a sign on it with huge letters saying: NO PLAYING IN THE CHURCHYARD.

We went on. Large clouds rolled calmly by above our heads, and higher up in the sky, long, veil-like wisps, like dirty white strands of fleece on a machine in a wool mill, looked as if they had been passed through a sieve. I pictured Godaleva, combing her hair in front of the mirror like a princess. My thoughts turned to her all too often. Even during a lull in the lessons, when the boys were solving a maths problem or writing an essay. I had to force her out of my mind so as to be able to concentrate on the lesson or marking work at hand. Marcus was silent. Looking at him from the side, I noticed his forehead was furrowed in a frown. Finally, he mustered the courage to ask me the question he had been mulling over.

'Sir, why do you go on walks all the time?'

'What else can a man do on his free days?'

'But you go out in the lousiest weather. My mother says so.'

'I've done it since I was a boy. In the woods. To see the wildlife. And because walking helps me think.'

'What do you think about?'

'Oh, all kinds of things,' I lied. 'About my lessons. About the exams I prepare for you. About you boys. And just life in general.'

'Aren't you happy with your life, then? If I think about something a lot, it's because I want to change it, because there's something I don't like.'

''Course I'm happy. Look at the great job I've got: making boys like you even cleverer.'

He smiled shyly.

'But what do you think about when you think about life?' The boy's tenacity was exactly what I liked so much about him. He wanted to understand things, didn't give up at the first hurdle. Nor the second. He would circle round, like a bird of prey peering down from the air, then suddenly focus all his thoughts on one question, one problem, going just that little bit further in looking for answers and solutions than other boys his age. He had a strong will to know and understand things, and took the time he needed. I felt an urge to tell him something essential about myself, but only obliquely, couched in a metaphor.

'Let me explain to you how I see life, Marcus: you're in a race. You pant and sweat, when all you really want is to give up, lie on your back in the grassy bank and look up at the birds, the butterflies and the blue sky. But you run on, as if you were being forced to. But no one makes you run the whole race. And as you run, your heart beats like mad, you taste beads of sweat trickling over your cheeks and into the corners of your mouth, you hear your heavy breathing. That's life. You can keep up with the other runners. But your thoughts are different from theirs. And then there's the runner in front of you—of course you never look back—who looks so much more athletic, runs with so much more ease and speed, is not the least bit bothered by the pebbles, the mud, the wind. He runs up ahead, or you are falling behind. Your body struggles, cramps, spits, but doesn't give up. Your thoughts have long since stopped following you. And just before he disappears from sight and you make a final effort to catch up with him, you suddenly notice the mark on his back: a thick, horizontal line. Then it hits you. Like a cannonball to the stomach, hurling you back to square one. The finishing line is an illusion. At that moment, your thoughts catch up with you, you rein in that body of yours and do what you had meant to do from the start: you lie down in the grass and stare up at the blue sky.'

I suddenly noticed that his strides were as long as mine and we were walking in step, even though I was two heads taller than him. As I watched our legs with fascination, I saw that his trouser legs were too long and too wide, so much so that only the shiny toes of his shoes peaked out and it looked as if he didn't have any feet at all, that they had sunk into the tarmac we were walking on—it looked like hard work.

'I think running is a boring, stupid sport,' he said.

It only occurred to me then how unfortunate my choice of metaphor had been, as Marcus had never been able to run a long distance, had never known the feeling of the body leaving the mind behind. His muscles and bones were not strong enough. He was more mind than body.

'So do I,' I said after a while, deeply humbled.

We walked past a cattle pool that was swarming with

mosquitoes. In the middle of it, a peeled tree trunk rose above the surface of the water.

'Can you swim, Marcus?'

'No.'

He saw me look at the pool.

'But I would really like to learn.'

We climbed over the fence, taking care not to snag our clothes on it. The water reeked. Green froth drifted up against the edge.

'I know where there's a really nice pond,' he said.

'You mean the one on the countess's estate?'

I had often walked past in the first weeks of September, peering in through the bars of the closed gate at the pond full of water lilies.

He nodded.

'But it's on private property.'

'I know a secret way in. And there's a spot in a kind of inlet under the bridge, behind the large weeping willows, that's invisible from the castle.'

'Another time, perhaps,' I said. But at that moment, I had already made up my mind to do it one day, and what was more, I had also resolved to teach Marcus to swim.

We arrived at Gallows Woods, on the border with Vlamertinge. The door of the Dirty Pail restaurant swung open and a short, stocky man tottered out, his wife holding him by the sleeve while trying in vain to shut the door behind her. The man didn't want to wait. Grumbling, he jolted himself free and waddled into the street. The woman finally managed to pull the door to and ran after him, her handbag dangling from the crook of her arm. The two of them started a flaming row in the middle of the street. That voice. That night in Forest Lane. The voice of the little bully. I would have recognized it anywhere. Vicious and shrill, like the yap of a bad-tempered Pekinese. Marcus couldn't keep his eyes off the man either. I realized he recognized him. More than that: feared him, or at least didn't want to be seen by him, as he suddenly quickened his pace. The row had died down and the woman was dragging the reluctant little bully along by his sleeve, to the only car standing in the car park in front of the restaurant. I asked Marcus if he knew him.

'He visits sometimes,' he said.

The woman opened the car door on the passenger's side and shoved him in. We heard him curse, and while she briskly walked round the back of the car to get into the driver's seat, he wound down the window and ranted at her. Only when she had started the engine did he realize she wasn't standing where he thought she was.

'He's a judge at Ypres court,' Marcus said.

'A friend of your father's?' I asked.

'They were neighbours as boys and went to school together. In Mr Verslyppe's class, but he's been dead a long time.'

And then he added, 'I think he's a strange man.'

We were almost at the sharp corner when we had to step into the grass for a moment to let the car pass. The woman kept accelerating too much and then hitting the brakes. The window on the man's side was still open and his arm dangled limply over the side. I could have sworn he grinned at us and stuck out his tongue as the car coughed and spluttered past. His head lolled from side to side each time his wife jolted the car forward and hit the brakes again. We waited until they had safely passed us before going on. But we hadn't walked twenty paces before we saw the car stop. The door flew open and the man was pushed out. He crawled to the grass on his hands and knees and vomited his guts out.

Back home, Marcus ran to the garden to find Spiney,

while I sat on the window sill at the front of the house. Ants were crawling in and out of a crevice in the corner where a chunk of concrete had been chipped off. An earwig hurried away in the opposite direction.

I only noticed Godaleva when she had already cycled past the boys' school. Gripping the handlebars with both hands, she didn't seem to care about keeping her bottom covered that day, not even moments before she reached the house and a particularly kindly gust of wind blew up her skirt to expose a white buttock. The image stayed in my mind for the rest of my life. She stepped off her bike unabashed, though with more deliberation, and leaned it against the hedge. We heard Marcus's voice come from the back garden. I told her he was looking after my hedgehog. She was radiant that Sunday morning as she sat down next to me on the window sill. I spotted two ants crawling under the fabric of her skirt. She pressed her knees together and leaned forward with her hands on them as if to relax her lower back. The heels of her shoes dug into the moss between the stones. I would gladly have stayed this way, sitting side by side in the winter sunshine without looking at each other or exchanging a word.

She had different plans, however, launching into a monologue about all kinds of trivial things, the longest I had ever heard her speak. She was usually more reserved, limiting her words to the bare minimum, but today, she shared her thoughts as freely as a farmer sowing seed, never giving her tongue or lips a moment's rest. I was happy to listen, even feeling quite honoured at the impression she gave of being able to speak freely in my company. The two ants shot out from under her skirt and into the hole in the corner as if racing each other. It almost seemed as if both insects wanted to lay claim on having been first to discover that mountain of nourishing flesh. The curve of her thigh on the sill was like a magnet to my eyes. I couldn't decide—should I tell her about my plan to teach Marcus to swim? If she didn't approve, I would have blown my chance to teach him. Better to keep quiet and do it in secret. But what if it made him ill? I suddenly noticed the silence.

'You're a dreamer,' she said.

'Why does Marcus always wear long trousers?' I asked.

She gave me a surprised look.

'Because he's never wanted any others.'

'I think everyone should get as much sun on their skin as possible,' I said cautiously.

'That's true,' she sighed. 'But no matter what I say or do, I can't get him to change them. Not since the time he got that sunburn.'

'I'll get him out of them,' I said. 'I mean, I'll get him to ask you for shorts one day.'

'I know what you mean,' she said with a giggle.

She wasn't convinced. Marcus may not have been the healthiest of boys, but he could be very stubborn. I asked her if she wanted to see Spiney too. Marcus would enjoy that. She pushed herself up from the sill and went ahead of me. She stopped short at the corner, so unexpectedly that I bumped into her. She turned around and before I could apologize, the flood welling up in her eyes overwhelmed me, pulling my legs from under me like a powerful wave. I quickly walked past her.

Marcus's legs grew stronger and his back straighter. The paleness also vanished from his face and was replaced by a tan the colour of a beechnut. Perhaps it only seemed that way to me, but the contrast with his former complexion was striking. Our walks kept getting longer too, and on some days we walked so far we could make out the hop fields of Poperinge. The posts and wire supporting the vines looked like a gigantic string instrument that had dropped from the hand of a god and bored itself into the soil of the West Flemish hills. And true to their ethereal origin, they were covered in golden cones stretching toward heaven every spring. That is to say, if Marcus had accurately described the colour—I myself hadn't seen the hop in bloom yet.

We saw Victor, sweeping a pile of dust into the gutter with a broom. When he saw us coming, he planted the broom in front of his feet and leaned on the handle. Marcus smiled at him, Victor winked. We were walking on the other side of the road. Victor called something I didn't understand, and Marcus answered jovially.

'Victor's a kind man. He saved my mother a few years ago,' he said once we had passed him.

'What happened?' I asked.

'Late one night, she was cycling back from Boezinge, because we have family there. She had a fall, quite close to your house.'

'And Victor found her?'

'Yes. She was lying in a pool of blood. She had hit her head and was unconscious. Victor found her, picked her up and carried her to the doctor. Without him, I wouldn't ... '

'She's still here, that's all that matters,' I said. 'And any-way, your mother doesn't just give up. I'm sure of it.'

He relaxed a little. I put my hand on his shoulder and told him good things about my mother.

'A mother is more important than a father,' he claimed when I had finished.

'Why do you say that?'

'They have to be, we've lain in their tummies for nine months. We've listened to their voices, heard their hearts beat. Felt the warmth of their hands.'

'That's true,' I said. My hand was still on his shoulder. I removed it, though he didn't seem to mind. We had reached the graveyard.

'Did you know I haven't been christened?'

'No, I didn't,' I said, surprised.

'Aren't you about to be confirmed?'

'Yes. But I need to be christened first, or I won't be allowed to. My mother didn't want me to be christened when I was born. She said I was very ill for a long time, and she was worried the water on my forehead would make it worse.'

'So there are two celebrations coming up,' I said, trying to sound cheerful.

He nodded excitedly.

'How come you don't believe in God?' he asked.

'I think the world is too cruel for there to be a just god,' I said. 'And besides, I've never yet seen him.'

'But love isn't something you can see,' he said.

'Yes it is, Marcus. When two people like each other, you can see it in the things they do for one another. Surely you've seen it between your father and mother?'

'Not really,' he said thoughtfully. 'My father always works outdoors, and when he does come in he's usually silent. They never do anything together.'

'That doesn't mean there's no love,' I said.

'So there *is* a love you can't see,' he said. 'That means God *can* exist.'

'Perhaps,' I answered calmly.

'My father and mother believe in God, too. We pray before every meal and before we go to sleep at night.'

I was watching the gliding flight of a buzzard circling high up in the air.

He followed my gaze.

'Look, Marcus. Just look at that magnificent bird soaring through the air with such grace, such dignity and serenity. And look over there. See that lonely weeping willow standing between those two fields? Look at its long, drooping branches. Soon they'll be covered in fresh green foliage again.'

He nodded.

'My god lives in those beings,' I said. 'In the heartbeat of the buzzard, in the sap coursing through the tree.'

He gave me a funny look, tilting his head toward me.

'In the colours of the butterflies you draw so beautifully,' I went on. 'And I'm so happy you can see it too.'

'That bird will die someday,' he said glumly.

'All part of life, Marcus.'

He stared at the ground at his feet, we had been standing still for a while.

'And it's nothing to be afraid of, either. It's the same as being asleep. And who knows, you may wake up in a completely different world.'

The thought clearly appealed to him.

FROM A DISTANCE, I could see Mr Vantomme's legs stretched out in front of him, and for once felt like stopping for a chat with the man. When I got closer, however, I realized he wasn't alone; a shrivelled-up little woman was sitting next to him on a stool. She was leaning her gaunt shoulders against the brick wall, hands folded in her lap.

'Good evening,' they said.

I stopped to greet them.

'Out walking again?' he asked.

I nodded.

'The schoolmaster walks for miles,' he explained to the woman. 'But then of course there isn't much else to do here for a young man like him.' He winked at her. She hardly moved. Her feet were wide apart, but her knees touched. Her calves were swathed in brown bandages. They looked as spindly and shapeless as the legs of a chair. Her arms where just as thin, and ended in knobbly knuckles and crooked fingers. In the rain gutter above our heads, two great tits started squabbling. When they had finally made up, they winged through the air to the roof on the other side of the road, where they immediately picked another argument. She lifted her head, revealing the crucifix that had been hidden underneath her chin.

'And he really does go walking. That's no lie,' he told her. 'He doesn't just go down the pub, like most blokes.'

Another wink in her direction, and again she didn't see it. She did nod this time—approvingly, it seemed.

'Mette is the granny of one of your lads,' Vantomme said. 'Marcus.'

That surprised me. Either farmer Verschoppen or Godaleva had to be the last in a long line—or a late arrival—because this creature was as old as the hills.

'She's Godaleva's mother,' he added.

Again the woman nodded without making a sound. I had the impression that even nodding was an effort, and probably painful.

'Marcus is a smart boy,' I said, louder than usual, in case she was deaf as well.

'It runs in the family,' she answered. Her voice was clear. Wizened as she may have looked on the outside, the sound ringing out from her throat like a bell had kept its girlish quality.

'Godaleva always was quick-witted. Too quick,' she said.

'Always the top girl of her year,' Vantomme agreed. 'Very clever. And you know what they say, don't you, schoolmaster? That a bloke should never choose a wife cleverer than he is. But most of those dunces don't realize it until it's too late.'

'Yes, that's life, eh ... ' Mette sighed.

'Everything was better in the good old days, eh,' Vantomme said with a grimace as he attempted to shift his leg.

'Certainly not,' she said emphatically.

I enjoyed listening to her voice, so much so that I felt an impulse to fetch a chair from inside and keep the two of them company—though I had to admit to myself that a sordid thirst for facts from Godaleva's life had something to do with it.

'But Marcus is a clever boy too, and I hope he stays healthy and well. Such a droll little fellow.'

Vantomme agreed, repeating what she said almost word for word.

'I hope so too,' I said.

'Remains to be seen, with a father like that,' she said bluntly.

Vantomme asked me if I wouldn't like to sit down. There wasn't another stool, but the tone of voice she used when talking about Marcus's father had sparked my interest, so I fetched a chair. The great tits were back in the rain gutter, squabbling again. Not with each other this time, but half a dozen sparrows that had landed too close. The shrill chirping hampered our conversation, and we watched the birds together. Just as Vantomme wanted to say something, a glob of bird dropping hit my eye. They looked at me, saw the white bird shit with the black kernel in the centre where my left eye should have been, and burst out laughing. She with a shrill cackle, he slapping his knees and gasping for breath. Embarrassed, I took out my handkerchief and wiped the shit from my eye.

'Besides the colour of his hair and eyes, Marcus does not seem to have inherited many traits of his father's,' I said.

'Just as well,' she said.

'Nor from his mother, when you think about it, eh?' Vantomme said, turning to Mette.

'They almost lost him. His heart just wouldn't start beating. And he was as purple as the Pope during Lent.'

'She only told me that much later,' she said.

'From the start, Verschoppen couldn't bear the fact that his own son almost died, and he still blames her for giving him an ailing child. At least, that's what she tells me on the rare occasions she visits.'

They were silent. I suddenly felt a tension, as if a glass dome had been placed over us out of nowhere, amplifying every sigh or look reverberating around in it.

'Well, that's life. Child-rearing, eh. Hardest job there is,' Mette said.

With those words, the tension melted away as quickly as it had descended on us. In an instant, they had forged a silent pact not to give me any more information. I stood up and said I should be going.

SPRING ARRIVED. The Sunday morning I guided Marcus into the water for the first time was remarkably warm for the time of year. I knew he was keen to learn to swim, in the spot he had chosen especially for that purpose: the pond on the countess's estate. That picturesque, peaceful spot under the red-brick bridge, invisible to passers-by.

'Do you want to get in?' I asked after we had contemplated the serene view for several minutes. He put his hand on my arm. His eyes sparkled. Seeing it filled my heart with an unaccustomed warmth. Marcus made a step forward and started to undress. He folded his clothes into a neat pile and put them on top of his shoes, which he had carefully placed side by side. I followed his example, casually telling him he would do better to wear shorts next time; there would be less risk of getting them dirty and of his father or mother noticing anything. I still hadn't discussed the swimming with Godaleva, though I saw her every Sunday morning. He nodded at my advice, too excited to give much thought to the inanity of my argument. Standing on the edge of the pond, the mud oozing up between his toes and the sunlight warming his bare upper body, he looked calm, and completely at home in this place of tranquil beauty. He couldn't take his eyes off the water. It looked like glass. I stood next to him, suddenly feeling uneasy. What if he caught pneumonia? Or worse? I would never forgive myself. Even before I could suppress my doubts about the swimming lessons, he took a deep breath, grabbed my hand and pulled me forward, into the cold water. At that moment, I could have sworn I heard footsteps behind us, the scrape of a thorn or twig catching on fabric. I turned round and peered into the thicket, but nothing moved. We could still go back. It was a mad idea. It was not up to me to teach someone else's child, who was already sickly, to swim. Another sound I couldn't place. What if someone saw us here? The thought hadn't even crossed my mind before. What would that person think? The touch of Marcus's fingers prodded me out of my reflections. The water reached up to his navel. He was shivering.

'That's far enough,' I said.

He wanted to go on. I pulled him back by his arm.

'Now, lie down on my arms,' I said, bending over and stretching out my forearms. 'You need to keep your body straight and practise the strokes first.'

He was a fast learner, but I soon noticed he was getting short of breath. Pushed down by his weight, my feet sank deeper and deeper into the mud until I was sucked in over my knees. The thought flashed through my mind that if he did something rash now, I might not be able to free my legs in time to help him. Marcus rested for a moment, lying still and staring at the water. I saw the pinkish, wrinkled flesh of his nape, felt his heartbeat on my arm. My arm started to cramp with the effort.

'Look! See the water over there!' he said, pointing to a spot beyond the bridge where the sun's reflection was overwhelmingly bright, contrasting sharply with the shade underneath. He shivered again. The goose bumps covering his skin reminded me of his fragile health.

'Come on, let's get out,' I said.

'No! Not yet!'

'Then carry on with the exercises,' I said. 'Or you'll grow cold.'

He diligently went back to work. The cramp in my arm eased. I lowered his body a little, just enough for him to feel the water push him up. The tendons in his neck tightened and his shoulder blades moved up and down with each stroke. After a while I decided to call it a day, dropped my aching arms and carefully guided him back to his feet in the water. I myself could hardly move. Wanting to help, Marcus grabbed my hands to pull me out, but my one foot slid out of the mud while the other was still stuck, and I lost my balance. He fell over backward. Panicking, I pulled free my other foot in a few moments, leapt over to him and lifted him up under his armpits. He calmed down, put his arms around my neck and his legs around my waist, clinging to me as I waded back to the edge of the pond. I could feel the moist warmth of his lips at my throat. I let go of him when I had reached our clothes, but he still held on to me.

'Marcus,' I whispered, as if to wake him up. He lifted his head, his face very close to mine, and eventually let go. I went back to my pile of clothes and dressed awkwardly. We didn't say much on our way home. He was tired.

We both froze on seeing farmer Verschoppen, not Godaleva, waiting for us at the gate in front of my house. Was she ill? Why wasn't he in the pub?

'Better not tell your father and mother about the swimming,' I said to Marcus. 'And perhaps you should wear shorts next time.'

He nodded without a word. Then he stopped and turned to me. We were about ten metres away from his father.

'Thank you,' he said. The confused look on his face worried me, and he was biting his lip. And he didn't ask to see Spiney again. Perhaps it was the exhaustion.

'Had a good, long walk?' Verschoppen asked. Marcus stared at his shoes. He stood further away from his father than I.

'Almost to Poperinge,' I lied. I could only hope it hadn't been his footsteps I'd heard at the pond.

'Wittering on about books and looking at creepy crawlies, no doubt?' Was he jealous? There was certainly contempt in his voice.

'We did indeed grasp the opportunity to learn something,' I said. It struck me that he might even appreciate my efforts to teach his son to swim, but I said nothing more.

'I often hear your name mentioned at the dinner table,' he said, his thin lips still in a tight line.

'Come on, we're going home,' he snapped at Marcus after staring at me for a few moments, a muscle twitching in his jaw.

'Didn't you come by bike?' Marcus asked in dismay.

'Bike? Never use the things. You know that.' he answered gruffly. Marcus heaved a sigh. The prospect of having to walk all the way home all but made him burst out in tears. I felt guilty. His father had already left without looking back. I seized the opportunity to whisper to Marcus that we wouldn't walk as far next time so we'd have a lot more time in the water. That is to say, if the weather was good. It seemed to cheer him up. He said goodbye, turned and lumbered after his father.

'**DAVID? ARE YOU** all right?'

'David? What is it?' I shot bolt upright in bed. Wide awake. A ray of moonlight illuminated the skulls and bones in the cupboard. The cow's nail, caked with dung, was at the exact centre of the beam. There was tepid, sticky goo between my legs.

'David!'

'Dammit, Ratface, be quiet. It's the middle of the night.'

I felt in my underpants with my hand, stuck a finger into the goo and pulled it back to examine it. It wasn't blood. Not brown, either. It glistened. Just like the snot I used to wipe from Ratface's nose when he was smaller.

'You were making funny, loud groaning noises.'

'I was dreaming,' I said.

'What about?'

'Don't remember exactly. Some animal or other, attacking me.'

'A monter?'

'I'll monter you in a minute if you don't shut up.' I was serious. I was angry. And afraid, and confused.

'Or was it Zaebos?'

I didn't answer.

'But David, that's such a long time ago. You should try not to think about it anymore.'

My nine-year-old little brother was consoling me.

'Yes. It was Zaebos,' I lied.

Then suddenly I remembered, felt the tips of her hair tickle my chest, her nails dig into my back.

'Go to sleep,' I told Ratface.

I stood up, took a towel out of the cupboard and quickly wiped myself with it. I knew he was watching me, squinting into the semi-darkness to see what I was doing.

'Did you poo in your bed from fear?'

'Of course not, dammit!'

'Sorry, David.' His voice sounded pinched.

'Be quiet and go back to sleep!'

I climbed back into bed and lay on my side, my back to him.

THE EASTER HOLIDAYS arrived and again the school closed its doors. Godaleva called round to tell me Marcus wouldn't join me on my walk on Easter Sunday. They had invited family for a meal after Mass. She also said that Marcus had been exhausted the Sunday before, and that it might be a good idea to take a break. If she had noticed how much healthier Marcus looked, she didn't mention it. I wanted to know why she hadn't come to pick him up last Sunday, but just managed to hold back the question. Hiding the disappointment in my voice wasn't as simple. She stood there, holding her bike. I asked her inside. She didn't have time. There were preparations to be made before the holiday. Would I be spending Easter with my parents? As I hadn't told her anything about my family yet, I forgave her the pain her question caused me. I shook my head. She gingerly leaned the bike against the hawthorn hedge and came up to me.

The last time I had been at Vantomme's to pay the rent, he told me that northern lights had been visible in Elverdinge on Wednesday the 15th of November, 1905. People had no idea what was happening. Some were terrified, thinking that Judgement Day had come, he said. Mette had even crept under the table, and his dog Penny had howled. It had happened at around six o'clock in the evening. Every star in the sky had sparkled that night. Then suddenly, red, green and pale yellow ribbons shot through the sky like spears of light. His poor memory notwithstanding, he remembered the spectacle as clearly as if it had been yesterday. But even if this divine, pagan miracle of colour had lit up the firmament at this instant, I would not have taken my eyes off Godaleva. It probably happened faster than it seemed, but it felt like ages before her body had come close enough for me to smell her scent. She put her hand on my arm, squeezed it, gave me a peck on the cheek. Then she was gone.

Lying in bed at night, I played the moment over in my mind. Had it been an instinctive, maternal gratitude for taking her frail offspring under my wing? Or something else? Something I did not even dare hope for? I should have been bolder, put my hands on her thighs and press her breasts to my chest while breathing through the hair tickling my nose. But I had suddenly remembered the fateful moment in which I had taken the initiative with Myrtha. So instead of acting on an irrepressible urge, I stood there like a sack of potatoes, displaying my complete uselessness. Afterward, I cursed my lack of forcefulness. I was, and always would be, a rat in a trap. Gripped by a sinister vision in which Godaleva's image merged with Myrtha and with Mother, both women digging their sharp nails into my skin—one with cruel intent, the other with wild abandon—I tumbled into sleep.

On the last Sunday of the Easter holidays, we went for another walk. Marcus was particularly lively that morning, and he was wearing shorts. He went to see Spiney before we left, chatting away to the hedgehog while feeding him worms. He got to his feet when I said I wanted to go. I told him we would walk toward Boezinge today. He straightened up. I noticed he looked different from when I had last seen him a fortnight ago. More spirited. Slightly more rebellious. It was a sign he was feeling more confident. He skipped ahead of me. Then he suddenly stopped, gave a pebble a hefty kick that sent it bouncing in the grass.

'I didn't draw any butterflies in the holidays,' he said.

'So what did you draw?' I asked in surprise.

'Take a guess.'

'A hovering falcon?'

'No.'

'A fox?'

'No.'

'You'll have to give me a hint, Marcus. The world's big, you know.'

'I drew a landscape,' he said. 'In colour.'

'The hop fields near Poperinge?' I guessed. He shook his head.

'Now I know,' I said. 'I'm certain.'

'Say it! Say it!'

'The pond with the white water lilies.'

'Correct,' he said, disappointed I had guessed so soon.

'What were you thinking of when you drew it?' I asked.

'I don't remember,' he said. He looked to the ground. I sensed he didn't want to tell me. I had the feeling that the bond of trust I had forged with him during our last walk had weakened.

'May I see the drawing?'

An irritable black-throated thrush belted out a warning from the top of a poplar tree.

'No,' he said, and skipped ahead.

In Stone Street, we saw a policeman. He was standing at the striped gate of a farm, lighting a cigarette. Walking past the gate, we noticed several other uniformed men in the courtyard. A fat officer with a drooping moustache was bellowing instructions, his voice booming out of the archway. The men loaded their guns. One had a rifle, which was cocked open, and stuffed two cartridges inside. The old farmer and his sons watched in dismay. The officer with the rifle stayed with them, as if guarding them.

'Bovine TB,' the man said when we stopped. He blew out smoke in between words. His cap was heating up his scalp, and the hairs above his temples were damp with sweat. 'All livestock is to be put down, and the dogs and cats. A shame, but it's very contagious.'

The men were dispersing. One of them went toward the dogs. I saw the sons kneeling down to say goodbye, fingers buried deep in the fur. The officer put a chain around the dogs' necks and dragged them behind the shed. Shots rang out. Then we were buried in an avalanche of gruesome silence. Marcus was crying. I pushed him on gently, away from the dismal scene.

The sun was already high in the sky, it promised to be a beautiful, warm morning. But Marcus's cheerfulness had vanished. At the pond, he undressed. He even took off his underpants. I watched him uncomfortably. He wasn't embarrassed. I had the strange feeling that he had become almost unaware of my presence, like a hunter who is so focused on his prey that he shuts out any distractions from his surroundings. He gazed at the water, mesmerized. When he started moving I realized he was about to go in on his own, and called to him to wait for me. He didn't hear me.

'Marcus!'

I quickly pulled off my shoes and socks, tossed my clothes on top of them, all without taking my eyes off him for an instant. He was in over his thighs. I waded in after him, through clouds of churned-up mud and sand staining the water that followed his body like a brown train. I grabbed his upper arm.

'You have to wait for me!' I shouted. The anger in my voice startled me.

'Marcus! Do you hear what I'm saying? Never go into the water alone! Never! Do you hear?'

He nodded absently. I scooped up some water in cupped hands and poured it over his shoulders. It had the desired effect. He wrapped his arms around himself. Bending my knees, I stretched out my arms for him to lie on. But he didn't want to, put his hand on my arm instead. He came closer, so close I could see the dark, downy hairs on his upper lip, the almost girlish upward turn of his long lashes. He was staring at me intently, his hands floating on the water as if they were too light to sink. And before I fully realized what was happening, he threw his arms around my waist and pressed a kiss on my chest. I shoved him away roughly. He stood in the water for several moments, frozen with shock. Then his head and shoulders slumped forward. I didn't know what to say, and was sorry for pushing him away with so much force. When he lifted his head again, he scowled at me, and beat the water with his hand. He turned round, stumbled and jumped, as far as the sucking sludge allowed it, to the middle of the pond. I watched as he sank ever deeper, until his feet hardly reached the ground enough to push off. It made him even angrier. Fuming and flailing his arms, he pulled himself forward. Then he fell over. I dove in after him. His foot slipped from my groping fingers. He was still trying to get away from me, kicking with all his strength. His heel smashed into my teeth. I finally managed to grab his foot, pulled him toward me and lifted him up. He started screaming and hitting. He kicked me in the balls with such force, I almost let go. Locking my arms around him tightly, I carried the raging and thrashing boy out of the brown water. When I had finally struggled out of the mud pool and put Marcus down next to his pile of clothes, I slapped him on the jaw. Harder than I had intended. He fell over backward. His legs and abdomen were covered in watery strings of mud. Then he started to laugh. I pulled him upright and shook him, until he threw his arms around me and nestled in mine, sobbing.

Godaleva was waiting for us. The closer we came, the clearer she must have seen something was wrong. We hadn't spoken a word on our way home. I wanted to tell him I didn't mind what had happened. But I couldn't get a word past my lips. Sensing his rage, I was afraid of saying something that would make him even angrier. When he realized his mother was watching our approach, he straightened up and jutted out his chin. Narrow as the pavement was, we had never walked at such a distance from each other. He clenched his teeth. His jaw muscle hardened. I realized with a pang of sadness that everything had changed, that what had been before would never return. He stood next to his mother. Before they left, Marcus did something that worried me: he held out his hand. His fingers felt cold and strong.

IT WAS A muggy summer's day in July, a few days before Ratface's tenth birthday. Myrtha and I were sitting on the grass in the shade of the hazel tree. She was wearing a dress with a red belt fastened tightly around her waist. I was sitting cross-legged beside her. Ratface was dozing off close by, his head resting on Cali's ribs. Scox was lying on the tiles in front of the screen door with his head straight up in the air, ears pricked up, then flat. I wanted to tell her everything: that I was in love with her. That I dreamed of her. But not that I ejaculated into a towel I kept beside my bed with ungovernable regularity. She moved her leg, stretched and lifted it, then crossed it over the other. The white shapes on the hemline of her dress had moved up a little. Her legs were long and tanned. Would I dare to put my hand on them? On the soft bulge of skin above her knee? Or better still, on her thigh, so I could slide it up. Under her dress. Up to her nipples. My balls ached. I pulled up my knees. Ratface came over and asked politely to use the toilet. She told him he didn't have to ask next time, and he dashed inside, slamming the screen door on Scox's nose. He ran to Myrtha with his tail between his legs and rubbed up against her. She put her hand on his scruffy head. The hand that could have been touching me. I wondered whether she suspected anything.

'Myrtha, I ... '

She looked up at me, blinking.

'What was it you wanted to say?' she asked when I hesitated. I could still back out of it, make up something else. It wasn't too late. Or I could let actions speak—weren't they supposed to be louder than words? In her case, especially. I'd never met such a decisive woman. At that moment, as if providence was trying to give me a hand, she turned away from me. She wanted to pick up the ball that was lying just out of her reach. Scox sprang to his feet. Twisting her hips, she leaned over as far as she could, the curve of her lower back and rump beckoning me irresistibly. It was forbidden. I did it anyway. My reckless hand already in mid-air between us. Action. Louder than words. At that moment, I placed my hand on her hip. Maybe she thought it was the paw of Scox, who was waiting for his ball, and didn't react.

Taking this for consent, I slid my hand over her side, up to her chest. She suddenly realized what was happening, turned round and hit me in the face, so hard I fell over backward. My head spun as I lay in the grass; the punch had been implausibly loud. Was I dreaming? Would I wake up in a moment with ejaculate in my underpants? Never had a punch to my head been so deafening. She started to her feet, eyes wide with alarm, standing motionless for a moment and tilting her head as if to listen. Then she crouched. For an instant, I thought she would pounce on me, but she leapt over me, ran to the kitchen, almost pulled the door from its hinges. I was still lying in the same spot. Scox and Cali leapt up against the door. Moments later, I heard her scream. I realized I must have done something terrible. I scrambled to my feet, half-stunned, not daring to go inside. She was singing. In a language I didn't know. It sounded wild and terrifying. I had to run away, home, back to my room as quickly as possible. Ratface? Where was he? I couldn't leave without him. I called his name.

His real name. 'Henri! Come here! Henri!' I suddenly realized he hadn't come back from the loo. 'Henri!' Mustering all my courage, I tiptoed inside. Through the kitchen. Down the hall. The door of the room was ajar. Her wails sounded menacing. I was terrified. Of her. Of what was going on in that room. Where was Ratface? I shuffled further, my back against the wall. Until I reached the door frame. Peered inside. She was bent forward on her knees. His white hair on her arm, against the black of her loose curls. Blood was leaking onto the tiles. My legs trembled. Then I saw it. The gun lying beside his hand. His fingers contracting and stretching spasmodically. She sensed my presence, called out to me not to come closer. I went in all the same. She was holding him in her arms. His face on her bosom. She was singing and cradling my little brother to his death.

JUST WHEN I thought I had found my place in Elverdinge as the teacher of the boys of Year Six, that I had discovered my worth in this life and had come to terms, as far as that is possible, with the death of my little brother, fate, in all its indifference, grabbed me by the collar and hurled me back into the dungeon of my past.

That Sunday evening was weighed down by a powerful thunderstorm. Sitting in my chair, I watched the lightning through the window, red bolts slicing up the darkness like razors. Almost simultaneously, thunder cracked the sky in two. Hailstones rattled against the window panes. I had never seen anything like it. It shook my house to its foundations. I tried to concentrate on the barn owl in the candlelight in front of me: black eyes in a white, heart-shaped face. Wings covered in speckles the shape of tears. In my opinion, no other bird exuded such calm wisdom as the barn owl. I had opened the book in the hope that it would distract me, as I had difficulty putting that morning's incident out of my mind. Then, unexpectedly, everything went silent outside. I snapped the book shut and stood up. The smell of the world after a thunderstorm—especially after a warm day that made the earth steam—had fascinated me even as a boy. Once all was quiet and I had drawn a few deep breaths, I decided it was bedtime.

My first thought was that the thunder had come back,

but I soon heard human voices between the thuds. Half-asleep and irritated, I climbed out of my trough and trampled downstairs. I missed a step. The crack was the last thing I heard. I don't know how much time had passed when I came round and found myself sitting on a chair like a naughty schoolboy, guarded by farmer Verschoppen and three police officers. Blood was trickling from my forehead into my lap. Buck was licking my hand.

'It's just a cut,' Verschoppen said.

They were holding my shoulders down. I still felt weak.

'Where's Marcus?'

I didn't understand the question, blinking into the light of a lamp.

'Where's Marcus?' he asked again.

'I don't know,' I said. The words consisted of more breath than sound. My lip was swollen, and when I ran my finger along my teeth, I noticed that one was missing.

An officer came down the stairs, treading carefully.

'He's not up there.'

'What's going on?' I asked.

The grip on my shoulders grew tighter. Verschoppen leaned over me. His voice was calm, but each word was a threat.

'Marcus is gone. He climbed out of his window.'

'He's not here,' I said, surprised.

My legs were still weak, but my mind was suddenly wide awake.

'The pond,' I said.

The officer with the white moustache came back from the garden, slamming the door behind him. He shook his head. The hands on my shoulders relaxed. Verschoppen was still standing in front of me, legs planted wide.

'What pond?'

'The one near the castle.'

'The spot next to the bridge,' I added. They didn't understand.

'Quick!' I shouted so loudly I made them jump.

'You stay here with him!' the officer with the drooping moustache barked at one of his men.

'I'm going too,' I said, standing up. I knew I could get there faster by climbing over the estate wall behind the church. A hand pushed me back into the chair. Farmer Verschoppen and the other officers had already run outside, and I could hear the metallic rattle of their bikes.

'It will take them even longer by bike, they'll have to make a detour to get through the gate,' I said in a panic to the man who was holding me down on my chair.

'You leave that to us, now,' he said, suppressing a yawn.

'But they might be too late, you numbskull!' I shouted.

He took out his truncheon and gave my shoulder a threatening tap. That moment, I sprang up, kicked him in the groin as hard as I could, shoved him to the floor where he lay in a groaning pile, and dashed outside. I leapt over a hedge, dove underneath a bell pull, ran along an endlessly long wall, through a back garden, over a fence whose iron pickets tore a piece out of my pyjamas, and rushed through the night like a ghost, through even more gardens, past coal sheds, outhouses, over hedges and fences to the countess's estate.

The last wall. Behind the church. Zigzagging between the crosses and tombstones. Behind the chapel in which bodies were gathering dust. It was a damned high wall. My fingers were bleeding. I lost my grip twice. Tried again. Searching for crevices between the bricks, deep enough to get a foothold. At last. I shoved in my foot. My fingers gripped the top edge of the wall just as my foot slipped off. Hanging on with one hand, I floundered about trying to get a hold with my other one. A sharp pang of pain shot through my shoulder. I swung to and fro, grabbed the edge, hauled myself up. I saw the beams of the bicycle lamps, heard the grunting and panting policemen. Buck rang alongside them, barking excitedly. He'd soon pick up my scent. For some reason, Victor's face appeared in my mind's eye. Perhaps I was hoping Victor would be Marcus's guardian angel, just as he had saved Godaleva after her fall. I pulled myself up and leapt down the other side of the wall, into the dark. I landed with a bump that made my knee crack.

The silence of the woods was awe-inspiring. I didn't dare go on. Afraid of what I'd find. Moonlight piercing the tree-tops here and there seemed to have marked a luminous path for me, straight to the water's edge under the bridge. I limped on, hearing nothing but my heavy breathing. At the last trees, I hobbled from trunk to trunk. They buttressed my body. The clearing. I looked. There was the pile, bathed in glorious moonlight: his neatly folded clothes on top of his shoes.

They found us. I was lying on my side in the sludge, my arms around Marcus. Buck was the first. He licked the vomit from my cheek. His muzzle sniffed at Marcus. He started to whine. Then the men came. Towering over us, blocking out the moonlight. Marcus was wrested from my arms. I wouldn't let him go, wanted to sink away into the mud with him. They bent over, sat on top of me and pulled my arms away. Verschoppen picked up the body of his son. Marcus's bare arms and legs dangling down, his wet hair draped over his father's arm. I was turned round. My hands were tied. A boot pushed my head deeper into the sludge, stopped when I didn't struggle. Then I was hoisted to my feet. They dragged me to the gravelled path and from there to the bikes at the gates of the estate. The last thing I saw was Verschoppen carrying his dead son into the night before a truncheon hit me full on the back of my head.

'HENRI?'

'Henri?'

'Brother, where are you?'

'I just wanted to tell you that your monter really does exist. He's stronger than a lion and a tiger together. If you see him, you must try to catch him. Tame him, by stroking him a lot. Talk to him. He will walk through the woods with you. He will be your protector. A better one that I was.'

I WAS LOCKED up in Ypres prison. The evidence against me was overwhelming. There were even witnesses. Besides, my signature stood at the bottom of a document in which I made a full confession. That's what the judge of Ypres court told me when he visited me in my cell. I was lying on a straw mat on the floor. It was the same man Marcus and I had seen vomiting into the grass on one of our walks. He of the disturbing sounds in Forest Lane. I listened, heard him speak, but his words washed over me. As if I were made of soap. I didn't say anything. That shrill voice. Indelible. Then he left. There wasn't a window to let in daylight. The little hatch opening and the hand shoving in my food were my only clues to whether it was night or day. But even that seemed doubtful at times. I ate little. I tried to make sense of what had happened, but my mind blocked every time I came to the image of Marcus's body. Then I'd see him, leaning against the playground wall, his body at the edge of the water, his hands and plump fingers. Then I'd hear his voice, his soft, rolling laugh that followed every correct answer given in class, and I'd have to gather my thoughts all over again. Calm down. Slow my breath.

Godaleva came. The clicking heels of her lacquered shoes echoed through the small room as she approached me with measured footsteps. The warden on duty had yanked me out of my cell. It was no place for a posh lady to visit, he said. She sat down, carefully placing her handbag between the legs of her chair. I stared at a brown stain on the table top.

'David, would you like to tell me what happened that Sunday morning?'

Her tone was flat. But when I looked up, I was surprised. I hadn't known what to expect: a woman whose hair had greyed with sorrow, a wrathful mother bent on revenge. But it was just Godaleva. I couldn't understand why there was no sign of pain or sorrow in her face. I told her all there was to tell: Marcus's wish to learn to swim and my half-hearted attempts to teach him. I omitted the kiss he had pressed on my chest.

'I'm sorry, Godaleva. I should never have done it. I don't know what I was thinking. He wasn't my child.'

'He was very happy on those Sundays,' she said. 'He looked forward to them all week.'

'I'm so sorry.'

'He told me, David. That Sunday after he had first gone into the water. I knew you were teaching him to swim. He was so happy and excited.'

So he had told his mother after all.

'I shouldn't have done it.'

'If I hadn't approved, I would have said so.'

'I absolutely forbade him to go into the water alone,' I said.

'He had grown stronger. In everything he did,' she said. 'Even in his thoughts. He had more willpower than before. He'd even started wearing shorts again.'

She swallowed. Her eyes welled up.

'I had no idea he would do such a thing, Godaleva,' I said.

'Neither did I. And I'm his mother.'

The image of Verschoppen carrying his dead son through the night suddenly came back to me. Where had he taken him? When was the first time she saw his lifeless body? And the last?

'You're not supposed to be here,' she said.

Maybe I was. I had given him the idea. I had made him stronger, enabled him to do what he had done: go into the water on his own.

'He worshipped you.' There was gratitude in her voice. She put out both her hands. I took them into mine. Soft and warm. She started to weep. I wanted to stand up, embrace her, but the warden prevented it.

'He loved you more than his own father.'

My next thought and emotion were oppressively bizarre. As if what she had just confided to me had caused a fertilisation, a germ planted in my brains, pollen stranded in a graveyard. Suddenly, I remembered the footsteps I had heard the first time I had guided Marcus into the water.

She bent over, took a handkerchief out of her bag.

'I'll see what I can do for you,' she said.

I nodded, lost in my memories. Then she picked up her bag, rummaged around in it and handed me a letter. The postman had given it to Mr Vantomme in confidence, who had passed it on to her. I absently glanced at the return address. My father. I put it on the table. The sound of her shoes didn't register anymore.

Some time after my meeting with Godaleva, two men stormed into my cell. They pulled me to my feet, pinned me to the concrete wall and beat me up. With their fists. With a stick. They didn't stop when I fell to the ground. Their kicks broke my ribs and arms. A large hand squeezed my throat. Then suddenly, they crept away. The floor of my cell felt soft. Instead of pressing down on the tiles, my broken bones lay cushioned in my flesh.

HIS NAME WAS Firmin. The tips of his white, drooping moustache almost touched. He sat on a chair in the corner of the room. I had lain in a bed in the Black Sisters hospital for over a month, strapped to splints on all sides so the broken bones could heal as well as possible. Not going anywhere now, Firmin said with a grin. He had been the one who found me, had in fact saved my life, as the jingling of his bunch of keys had chased away my attackers. A couple of nuns shuffled past pushing a cart full of jugs, poked their heads round the door, saw that everything was as it should be and shuffled on. They were used to seeing Firmin every day, sitting on the creaking chair in the corner in his prison officer's uniform. And when he wasn't there, someone else was. But that was only at night. At dawn, Firmin was back. I liked him.

'There's something brewing in Europe,' he said one morning as he walked into my room, which was bursting with sunlight.

It was July and the summer holidays had started. I was reminded of my boys. The nuns had looked after them until the end of the school year. They must all have received their Confirmation by now. Wearing shorts, and starched white shirts with bowties. I longed to see them again. To sit at my desk and tell them all about what had happened. Explain. Talk about their friend Marcus. Show them his drawings. Tell them his method of catching and drawing butterflies. That everyone deserved a second chance.

'It all started with that Austrian they bumped off over in Sarajevo.'

Firmin sat down with a sigh. He tossed his cap on the little table, knocking over a vase. The flowers, which had long since wilted, spread out in a perfect fan-shape on the floor. The sisters heard the crash and came in a little later, grumbling, to sweep up the pieces. Firmin watched their swaying backsides.

'The Belgian army is even mobilizing schoolboys now. I heard them get on the tram last night, making one hell of a racket. Glad I've only got daughters. There's tough times ahead for young men,' he said.

The doctor came in. After pulling and prodding my limbs, he decided they were healing well. But there wasn't much he could do about that missing front tooth. He winked at Firmin. Firmin chuckled, and said that since I hardly ever talked or laughed, the gap in my mouth wasn't noticeable. The doctor said I'd soon be able to go back to my cell. Firmin must have seen the fear in my eyes, for as soon as the doctor had gone, he told me not to worry. He would make sure no one would be able to get into the prison that easily a second time, and waved away my argument that one of the men who had beaten me up had to be a police officer. An investigation had been launched, he said. I should put my trust in it.

A loud rap on the door and there they were: Jef and Roger. I couldn't believe my eyes. They had cycled to Ypres on their own. I was touched. Standing at my bedside, they glowed with health and life. Jef's hair, which had always resembled a bird's nest, was cropped short. Roger looked as mischievous as ever, but he had grown, his crown just reaching Jef's shoulders. They were nervous, perhaps a little shocked at the sight of their broken and strapped-down teacher. I pretended not to notice, and produced my first smile in a long time especially for them. I saw their eyes slide down to the gap where my tooth had been. Jef said that the other boys had wanted to visit me too, but their parents hadn't allowed it.

'What were the nuns' lessons like?' I asked.

'We had to pray at the beginning of each one, and at the end, too,' Roger said.

'And go to confession every Friday,' Jef said.

'On our bare knees, on the hard boards.'

I smiled again. So did Firmin.

'And Roger was given a belting,' Jef said with a grin.

'What for, Roger?' I asked.

'Because I said that confession didn't work, that it only made us do more bad things.'

I felt a certain pleasure hearing how Roger had internalized my words. He did have a question, though.

'But sir, if someone has done something bad, surely that person can't go to heaven anymore?'

I could have confused them again by repeating that heaven didn't exist, but I didn't want to. I realized the nuns had done a thorough job.

He hadn't finished.

'But if that person goes to confession and says his Hail Marys and Our Fathers, what then? Can he go to heaven? And if that is so, surely he can just go on doing bad things? And then go to confession again?'

Firmin frowned. I could tell he was curious to hear my answer by the way he leaned forward.

'The Catholics have found a very clever remedy for that,' I said.

Marcus had explained it to me once. I felt the teacher within me surface, and for a moment I felt as if I were facing the class.

'If you have lead a good life, you go to heaven. But if you did something bad, you don't immediately go to hell. You are cast into purgatory first, and after you've been there for a long time, God might decide to send you to heaven. But only if you never did any more bad things—if you did, you're sent to hell after all. That's their solution.' I said.

Firmin leaned back again with obvious satisfaction. The two boys nodded as they let my explanation sink in.

'But I don't suppose you've come all this way to ask me that?' I asked.

Jef looked at Roger, who handed me the parcel he had been holding all that time. He realized I couldn't open it, but hesitated to do it himself. I nodded at him. His fingers ripped through the brown paper. I was touched when I saw what was inside. Two exercise books of Marcus's. One with exercises he had done and the other full of his drawings. I tried in vain to swallow the lump in my throat. I had to pull myself together. Jef and Roger had gone quiet. I wanted to hug them, to put my hands on their shoulders—instead, I looked at the two boys at my bedside and knew that after that day, I would never see them again. They would cycle home in the glorious sunshine, the summer's breeze in their faces, and carry on with their lives. And one day, when they were old and worn out, playing cards with their grandchildren on their laps, they might remember that strange teacher of theirs, Mr Verbocht.

Firmin had gone home. The remnant of daylight in my room was losing its battle against the gathering dusk. The footsteps of the night sister who had just passed died away. Marcus's exercise books were lying on my lap, in the same place Roger had put them. My mind wandered back to the first Sunday morning I took him to the pond. I could hear the footsteps, the scratch of a thorn against fabric, the snapping twig, with increasing clarity. Those three sounds drowned out all others in my recollection of that morning. There were too many for them to have been imaginary. Who had been spying on us? Was I looking for a perpetrator because I didn't want to believe that Marcus had committed suicide? Or for a witness who would know I was innocent? I should never have shoved Marcus away from me like that. I cursed, looking at the crucifix above the door. The faces of my mother, Myrtha and Godaleva floated before my eyes, followed by those of Father Storme and farmer Verschoppen. They all pointed at me, sneering, calling me names.

The chains rattled when I tried to pick up the exercise books. I attempted to sit up, pulled myself up by my arms despite the pain. I wasn't able to do even that. My head and shoulders dropped back into the pillow. The ghosts' index fingers touched the tip of my nose. The jeering and cursing swelled into a clamour of noise that exploded in my face and ears. I tried to calm myself—I could feel it coming, the avalanche of raging madness that was gathering momentum deep inside—but it broke loose, with a power I hadn't known was in me, making the pain in my body dwindle into insignificance, pulling the chains out of the plaster of the ceiling. Whirling up through my throat, it spilled, screaming, from my clenched jaws, blowing bubbles in the foam at my lips. Until madness itself forced my mouth wide open and tore out in all its diabolical fury.

I was taken away. Four black sisters pinned me down. Delirious, I was wheeled down white corridors, when Marcus suddenly appeared to quench my thirst with a mug of ice-cold water. Underneath the majestic crown of a beech tree in the woods I knew so well, I was leaning against the bark, my little brother beside me. On either side of us lay dead deer with ripped-out bowels. Then I was being kissed and stroked by Godaleva, the tip of her tongue in my ear. My father held a solemn speech, dressed in his suit. Beside him, Myrtha's head on a chopping block. My mother undressing and washing me. Her greasy strand of hair tickling my belly. A veil of cold metal around my head. My mouth pried open, pills shot in through a plastic tube. I shivered. The room shook. I strained at the straps, panting. I spewed. Floated. Fell. Further and further down. Mother! Mum!

Godaleva came back. She had been visiting me all the time, she said. Ever since the moment I had been allowed to have visitors. That had been two months ago. She always stayed an hour. I was usually asleep because of the powerful sedatives, but I would wake with a start every so often and look around the room with wide-open eyes without recognizing her or the place I was in. If I didn't calm down again immediately, she would have to call a sister who would then come storming into the room, tear away the sheets and stick a syringe into my buttock. I had also been talking in my sleep. About Ratface. My mother. About Marcus and about her. She said it in a timid voice, as if she felt guilty for involuntarily eavesdropping. She wanted to be completely honest with me. I reassured her. If anyone should be allowed to hear it, it was her. She laughed nervously, folding the white sheet between her thumb and index finger, and put a hesitant hand on mine. I was shocked to hear how much time had passed without my noticing. It wasn't always easy to visit, Godaleva said. The Germans were entrenched around the city. The hospital would shortly be evacuated and even the patients in this wing would be moved to a safer place. I knew that by 'patients in this wing' she meant the lunatics of the hospital. She was so glad I had finally come round. She also told me, with apparent indifference, that farmer Verschoppen had left home months ago. He was serving as an officer, stationed near Kemmel. I had the impression that his absence came as a relief to her, giving her the space she needed after Marcus's death. It didn't occur to her he might be killed.

'I talked to you, too,' she said.

I hauled my body into an upright position, stuffing the plump pillow with the yellowish drool stains behind my back.

'I didn't hear anything,' I said.

'Just as well.'

She looked at me, head tilted to one side. Then she said I looked different from before. Her fingers were still covering my hand like a warm blanket. She bent over, her face so close I could see her chapped lips, smell her breath: mint, with a hint of sweetness. Perhaps it was the missing front tooth, she said. Or maybe the threateningly confident look in my eyes. Looking into them felt like looking down the barrel of a gun, she said. I didn't tell her about the criminal fantasies and bloodthirsty nightmares I had lived through during my medicine-induced sleep, and which were still vivid in my memory. Delusions, which I could not shake off even now I was fully conscious, but which seemed to sprout from me like fungi from a mouldered tree trunk: retaliation for the prison thrashing, for incarcerating an innocent person, revenge on farmer Verschoppen for never understanding his son and for not giving me a lift in his cart when I was carrying home my coal scuttle. Even my mother didn't go unpunished. And running through the violence like a thread was the image of me, wearing a halo of righteousness, like an angel of vengeance. A feeling that evaporated as soon as I realized that none of all that would actually take place.

'What kind of things did you tell me?' I asked.

'That I was once a patient here, too.' She scrutinized me,

as if she was afraid of the consequences of her words.

'Then we have even more in common than I thought,' I said. She smiled faintly, aiming her gaze at the gap between my front teeth.

'I was addicted for a while. During and after my pregnancy with Marcus. To laudanum.'

Hearing his name from her lips was torture to me.

'I was in so much pain, David.'

She started weeping silently. I then did something I had been aching to do for so long. I pulled her to my chest. Her ear on my heart. My chin on her blonde bun. The hairpin with the carved butterfly wings pricked into my Adam's apple like the point of a knife. We stayed like this for some time. I pressed a kiss on the smooth, fair skin behind her ear.

'I made him ill. It was my own fault,' she said.

'You don't know that,' I said soothingly.

'I should have been stronger. But the pain was unbearable. And my husband never could forgive me. I could always see the accusation in his eyes. He refused to accept that his son was not healthy. He raised Marcus with a firm hand, made him work hard. To drive out the weakness, he always said.'

'I know.'

I could hear it as clearly as if Marcus were shovelling coal in the next room: the rattling cough.

She stood up, felt at her bun, and through the water brimming in her eyes she saw the dent her hairpin had left on my throat.

'Sorry,' she said, rubbing my Adam's apple with the tip of her finger.

'Where is Marcus buried?' I asked once she had calmed down and taken up her usual dignified position next to me, clutching the crumpled lace handkerchief in her fist.

'In the furthest corner of the graveyard. Under the large chestnut tree. He always loved that place.'

I knew the spot, it was surrounded by a hornbeam hedge that kept its green foliage even in winter. I had also wondered why it was separated from the rest. Marcus could undoubtedly have told me.

'Father Storme refused to bury him on consecrated ground.' I looked at her in surprise.

'Marcus had not been christened yet,' she said. She seemed to feel guilty about that, too. I remembered talking about it with him during one of our walks. He was very keen on getting baptized. I didn't mention it to Godaleva.

'Besides, he committed suicide, though that was not the reason they wouldn't bury him in consecrated ground—they still think you had something to do with it.'

She started crying again. Suicide. A twelve-year-old boy. Almost thirteen. It was inconceivable. The thought of it again turned my stomach inside-out, skinned my heart. And again I thought of the footsteps I had heard. I didn't mention them, either. I couldn't find the words to console her.

'What will happen with you now?' she suddenly asked out loud, taking hold of my hand again.

'I don't know, Godaleva.'

'I know someone. A friend of my husband's. He's a judge. I'll pay him a visit,' she said, almost tripping over her words in her combativeness.

I remembered the judge. The man who lay vomiting on the side of the road. The little bully with the shrill voice in Forest Lane, whom Marcus had wanted to avoid. And he knew that I knew.

'Don't do that, Godaleva.'

'Why not? I want to help you.'

'I know, and I am grateful to you for it, but they'll see

sense once they investigate the case thoroughly.'

'Thoroughly? David! There's a war going on! Do you really think they will make time to prove your innocence? Maybe they'll just leave you to rot in a cell until the war's over, and who knows how long that will be?'

'Then at least I'll be safe,' I said with a forced grin, realizing too late that my lips were exposing the gap in all its glory.

'In any case, I won't leave you in the lurch,' she said as she stood up and slipped the strap of her bag over her shoulder.

'Godaleva, please. I can take care of myself.'

She looked down at me. The loose strand of blonde hair, the curly end of which had to tickle her cheek. The skin of her throat, so pale pink and taut. She would not be out of place gliding between the water lilies on the sparkling surface of the pond I had lowered her sickly son into.

'No. No, you can't,' she said, bending over to kiss me goodbye.

IN LATE JANUARY 1915, I was taken back to my cell. Fully recovered, according to my papers. Ready to be tried, and serve my sentence as a healthy man. It didn't take them long. The judge honoured me with a personal visit. His eyes glinted with satisfaction, even though I had never harmed the man. He tried to sound intimidating, but was thwarted by his shrill voice.

'In times of war, martial law applies,' he said.

Since the national interest took precedence over my case, it had been adjourned until after the war, even if it lasted half a lifetime. His lips curled in anticipation. There he stood, only the bars between us, his short, fat body oozing triumph. His paunch squeezed in by an indestructible belt. Seeing it, I heard the jangle of its metal buckle between the trees. The words shouted out in the heat of battle. Suddenly, I roared with laughter, and had to hold on to the bars to keep my legs from giving way beneath me. He recoiled, bewildered, but was soon fuming with rage and hissed, 'Don't you believe you can wait out your time here in safety. They're coming to get you tomorrow. You're going to the front.'

A malicious glee appeared on his face at this prospect, but when he realized his words made no impression on my laughing fit, he clenched his jaws, opened the briefcase he had placed on the floor next to him and hurled the documents in through the bars. At that moment, I noticed a presence behind him. A shadow, hidden behind the protruding wall of the corridor about five metres away, the one spot the light didn't reach. The judge's mouth opened to say something more, but he jumped when the shadow suddenly stepped into the light and stood behind him. Firmin. Saying a nervous goodbye in Firmin's general direction, he eventually picked up his briefcase and hastened toward the metal door at the end of the corridor. Firmin watched him until he had disappeared from view.

'Bad news that, eh.'

'I prefer the front to prison, Firmin.'

'You don't know what you're saying.' There was compassion in his voice.

'That's true,' I answered. All the same, I was curious about the future.

'So many good young men have already fallen,' he said, giving me a sad look.

His pity left me unmoved.

'I don't believe you're guilty,' he said. 'You're no murderer. I've seen them. The real murderers.'

'Thank you, Firmin.'

'The military police will come for you tomorrow,' he said, as if to confirm it. I nodded. Then he put his hand through the bars. I gave it a long, firm shake.

Strange as it may sound, and even though I could hardly imagine what was in store for me, the prospect of fighting in a war brought me peace. When you're dead, you're dead. And if I was spared, I would live on in the knowledge that Godaleva believed in my innocence, and even, I dared claim, liked me. Basking in that blissful feeling, I fell into a peaceful sleep.

When I woke up early next morning and leaned against the bars to look at the wintry morning light in the corridor,

I noticed the door of my cell was half open. I could escape! No one would stand in my way. Perhaps I'd find a pile of civilian clothes put out for me on a table somewhere. Or sandwiches wrapped in brown paper, and a canteen full of beer on top. All the necessary forged documents. I pulled the door to.

The army pickup truck was idling with two wheels on the pavement. There were a number of men inside already. They watched me suspiciously as I climbed in. I sat down in the only free spot, against the tailboard. No one was in uniform, and I concluded they all had to be fresh recruits—volunteers perhaps, men with an aversion to cowardice who had finally found their purpose in life. Some held overstuffed suitcases between their feet, others carried knotted knapsacks over their shoulders. The man in front of me had delicate hands emerging from intricately embroidered shirt cuffs. He looked as if he were on his way to a party rather than a war. I was the only one with no luggage, and I was wearing prison clothes.

No one said a word. Driving for hours over winding, pot-holed roads, we sometimes heard the roar of distant cannons and saw *Taube* aircraft ominously silhouetted against the sky, but above all, were tortured by an excruciating pain in our backsides from bumping up and down on the hard floorboards. The smell of petrol in the back of the truck was making me feel sick. Someone spewed his breakfast onto the rusty metal of the floor. White, mushy chunks.

All of a sudden, the driver hit the brakes. We bumped up against each other, involuntarily fending off each other's arms before shuffling back over the slippery planks, embarrassed. On arrival at the *centre d'instruction* number 7 at Camp d'Auvours in northern France, we were immediately divided into groups: the burly men to the Artillery, the light ones to the cavalry and the tough ones to the infantry. Instead of uniforms, we were issued with linen waistcoats and trousers, which we had to wear over our other clothes. We slept on straw-filled sacks in white, conical tents.

I adapted to the order and discipline of the training without problem, but not the icy cold just before sunrise. I had the feeling I had entered the second act of my life. That I was given a second chance. A life which would allow me to play a more manly and decisive role, to erase myself, purge myself from everything that had gone before, and in which my sole aim would be survival. I myself was surprised at how completely this thought dominated my heart and mind. I did the work that was expected of me without grumbling. I was the first of the men to learn how to handle a Mauser, how to load, reload and clean it. I marched, shoved my bayonet into the sacks to the hilt every time and excelled in the drills the sergeants put us through. The envy of the others was like a blade in my back. I knew they kept an eye on me, what they thought of me. They wanted to break me before I would be sent to the trenches. But I didn't care. I was no longer interested in friendship.

Four months later, I was a fully trained foot soldier: hardy and tough, ready for battle. I could hardly imagine my former life as a teacher anymore, though the faces of the boys would still sometimes pop into my mind in unguarded moments. One by one, like a row of chiselled busts in a museum, as if someone had dragged a duster across the chalky blackboard of my memory. Mother no longer penetrated my dreams. Neither did Myrtha. Spiney, on the other hand, regularly appeared before my mind's eye in full detail. His image would come to me out of the blue, on seeing a little brown heap in a field during day-long marches, or when a chunk of lard in the soup I was eating reminded me of a slug. A fox's trail in the snow, the lonely dawn song of a blackbird, the countryside in frozen silence invariably turned my thoughts to Ratface and Marcus. Strangely enough, however, the pain I had always felt at those memories had gone. And then of course there was Godaleva. Her face seemed sewn to the inside of my eyelids, closer than the others, but blurred.

THE ARMY CHAPLAIN, a tall man wearing a grey woollen cap, was standing at the door of his chapel one day as I walked past on my way to the latrine. He knew my name.

'Private Verbocht.'

He waved me closer, in the same way I used to wave to the boys if they misbehaved on the playground. I went up to him, wondering what this man wanted to talk to me about. He had probably noticed I always sat in the last row during the compulsory services, that I didn't go to communion or do the offertory, and was even less inclined to open my mouth to sing. His chin was split like a deep ravine, two walls of flesh parted down the middle like the waters of the Red Sea by Moses. (Another story Marcus had told me.)

'There's been talk about you,' he said. His tone was not disapproving. It sounded more like an account of something he had registered.

Rubbing the stubble on his chin with his hand, he let the tip of his index finger rest in the cleft and fixed me with a stern look. He was clearly not expecting a reply, as he immediately went on.

'They are impressed by your fervour, your precision, your physical condition. You appear to be talented. A first-class soldier.'

I stared at my shoes. At the crust of mud on the toes.

'That's good,' he said. 'Very good.'

'Thank you,' I muttered.

'Very good. For a soldier,' he said.

I started to feel uneasy, didn't understand what he was getting at. And I urgently needed to go to the loo.

'But I would like to get to know the man behind the soldier,' he said. 'You used to be a teacher in Elverdinge, did you not?'

'Yes.'

He nodded. I didn't like the direction this conversation was meandering into.

'I bet you were a good, conscientious teacher,' he said.

'I like to think so,' I said gruffly.

I deliberately turned my head to go on, but none of the silences between his questions was long enough for me to slip away. In the distance, a kestrel was hovering above a field, the black band at the end of its fanned-out tail like a smile suspended in mid-air.

'Do you realize it is very likely that you will soon take the life of a human being, Private Verbocht?'

'I do. Though I'd rather not think about it,' I answered truthfully.

'That's what you've been taught, of course. Not to think too much about anything, neither now nor later, or you'll go mad,' he said. 'That's a soldier's answer. I wish to hear the answer of the teacher. Of the man who stood in front of children every day, who taught them various subjects with an eye toward their future.'

'That man no longer exists,' I said.

'The soldier is the one who will kill, but the man will have to live with it afterwards.'

'If I survive.' I said it with complete indifference.

'Don't misunderstand me,' the chaplain said, stroking his stubble. 'I don't want to sow doubt. There is more than one hell awaiting you. You will have to do what you've been trained for. But you should reflect on it, while you still have the chance. On the immense value of life, no matter whose it is.'

'This is not a good moment for reflection,' I told him. The pressure on my bowels was getting so strong I had to pinch my hole shut. Besides, we would be sent to the front in a week's time.

'Tell me why you don't believe in God.'

It was the last thing I felt like doing at that moment. But it sounded like an order, so I decided not to beat around the bush. 'The way I see it, faith in God is like a white dove bathing in a muddy puddle,' I said. 'I admit it contains a kernel of truth I can relate to, but it is corrupted and mutilated by its representatives, who use every opportunity to let their words and images detonate like bombs among the frightened people.'

He lifted his grey eyebrows. They were as rough and bushy as the bristles of a brush.

'No. I don't believe in it in the way that you advocate in your weekly services. Nor in mumbling Latin texts, swallowing stale bread, or the pressure of cold metal against my jaw.'

My eyes slid over to the kestrel, which was now falling from the air like a brick. I had a strange sense of feeling its heart beat behind its breastbone and the blood race through its veins, hearing the wind rush through its feathers, seeing the talons and beak, ready to strike in lethal unison.

'There is war. There is illness. There is manslaughter and suicide,' I went on.

It sounded like a refrain. A piece of poetry in the wrong place, at the wrong time. The kestrel rose, a rat struggling in its talons. He stared at me, shocked at the venom in my voice. He had kindled a spark of anger in me. My body was suddenly bathed in a scorching heat, as if my uniform contained a burning pyre. I asked him what he thought about the Omnipotence, Omniscience and Omnibenevolence of his God. The tremble in my voice irritated me. My breath was laboured. I had to get hold of myself, not revert to the ravings of a madman. Then it would all have been for nothing, my second chance wasted.

'As a lowly man, I am not to think about those things,' he said. 'God is unfathomable. We must trust in Him.'

'That's lazy and cowardly,' I snapped. 'Your God, if he resembled a human being at all, would be able to set everything right with a snap of his fingers. But he can't be bothered. So he's not omnibenevolent. Or perhaps he wouldn't be able to rid the world of human misery even if he wanted to. Then he would not be omnipotent. Or perhaps he's neither able to nor wants to. Then he's nothing at all. But the way you describe your God, he is both able and willing. In which case, my question is: why doesn't he do anything?'

'We must trust in Him.' That was his refrain.

'Well, mister chaplain, I may be young, but my life experience has already knocked out that trust in the first round. And it's not about to stand up again.'

'Faith is a matter of inner resilience.'

'So are my bowels, Father. Forgive me if I expelled myself from your God's church, though I never actually belonged to it in the first place, but I really have to go now. I have other things to expel.' I walked away quickly. I knew I had gone too far. He outranked me, and could not let this blasphemy—but especially my disobedience, as I had left without being dismissed—go unpunished. But I felt satisfied and calm.

The kestrel had disappeared.

I spent the rest of the week in prison, peeling potatoes and sewing mailbags, but not before I'd taken a good dump.

Elverdinge, the 14th of February, 1915

Dear David,

I hope this letter reaches you. I am sorry I haven't been able to say goodbye to you; when I went to the prison in Ypres, Firmin told me they had taken you away. I pressed my husband's friend, Judge Beaucourt, for help, but he said there was nothing he could do for me because of the war. I want you to know I did what was in my power. I cannot tell you how terrible I feel about the way you've been forced to go to war. Please don't lose heart. Take care of yourself, so you can come back.
I've been meaning to tell you that, on one of my visits, a man was sitting at your bedside while you were sleeping. I had never seen him before. He was wearing a smart suit and was holding your hand when I came in. He said he was your father. He told me about you as a child: strong-willed, always buried in a book, and that you loved animals. He also told me about your younger brother. I'm so sorry. I'm glad I've come to know a little more about you, but there is so much more I want to talk to you about. Please come back.

Love, Godaleva

A fortnight later, I was at the front, in the company of other godless men. Men as tough as old boots who couldn't see any further than the sights of their guns. I was to replace a fallen comrade. No one asked me who I was, where I came from, what I had been in a previous life or whether I had gone to Mass on Sundays like a good boy. I probably wouldn't make it to the end of the month, anyway. That part did interest them, as they'd put a wager on it. They were hard-nosed, foul-mouthed veterans who reeked like wet dogs and had probably been born fully fledged soldiers. They cursed and raged, thrived on the noise of shrieking bombs, fought among themselves but went to any length to protect each other in the face of the enemy. There was no room for a novice. Their indifference was a relief. But after a while, two men from Elverdinge, the Vermeulen brothers, started spending time with me—partly out of necessity, as we shared a dugout. When they told me which farm they came from, I realized I'd seen them before: they were the men standing in the courtyard of the farm Marcus and I had passed on our last Sunday walk, who had watched in dismay as the police officers slaughtered their animals. One of the brothers, Jef, was in love with a girl called Lora. He wanted to propose to her when he returned from the war. But she rented a room in the notary's house and all kinds of rumours did the rounds about her. He hoped they weren't true. He said the notary collaborated with the Germans and that he'd teach him a lesson one day. He wanted to impress Lora by learning to write, then he would be able to declare his love for her in a highly original way: by love letter.

We set to work, and for many evenings, when the bombing subsided and the distant night sky was a magical blaze of burning, blood-red bedlam, when the moon shone and we weren't digging tunnels like human moles, I taught him to write the letters of the alphabet.

'THERE'S SOMETHING FUNNY stuck in that tree over there, Schoolmaster. Can you see?'

My eyes followed his pointing arm. The tree stood in a snow-covered field like a birthmark on white skin. My company had arrived in the vicinity of Zonnebeke a few days earlier.

I had survived the first month. The veterans lost their bets. Only one man had put money on me lasting the month. He had looked me up and down and walked away without a word. Now he was standing next to me, a veteran of three wars: Sergeant Alois. Afterwards, when he had gone round with his helmet like a beggar to collect his spoils, he'd come up to me with a grin and said he'd been able to tell I was a survivor. It was all he had to say on the subject.

Four months had passed in the meantime. I was the only soldier in the company to be accepted by the veterans. They had noticed I was teaching the Vermeulen brothers to write, and wanted to learn, too. It must have been a sight to behold for the French officer who leapt into the trench that evening, baffled to see the indomitable veterans sitting in a row like schoolboys, each with the blank side of a letter on his lap and clutching a pencil stub in his right hand. Pale with rage, he started shouting orders, but not one of the men obeyed. They held slightly more privileges than ordinary soldiers. I was the only one who leapt to attention. Sergeant Alois nodded at me, and I provided the officer with an explanation. He strongly disapproved of my lessons, saying that at this time of day, there should be one of only two things in our hands: a shovel or a weapon. No one took any notice of him, and when he finally slunk away, the lesson continued as if nothing had happened. From that moment on, they called me 'Schoolmaster'.

'It can't be a branch,' I said to Sergeant Alois. 'Too straight. And it gleams.'

I estimated the tree was roughly one hundred metres away. The Germans had entrenched themselves on the crest of the hill behind Zonnebeke. They had won ground by poison gas attacks, and were now building concrete bunkers and installing a line of machine guns a few metres apart. By daylight, we'd walk straight into the sights of a sniper.

'We'll take a look tonight,' Sergeant Alois said.

From my first day in the platoon, I had never let the veterans catch even a whiff of fear on me. I followed on their heels like a bloodhound no matter the situation, and my willpower and determination were unrivalled. They didn't forget the speed of my reactions, which had more than once saved the life of one of them. Nor how I had slit a German's throat with a bayonet in front of their eyes, giving the blade a slight twist, just as I'd learned at Camp d'Auvours. He was the first German I'd fought in close combat. A man of average height with curly hair and a beard. His eyes bulged as we rolled over each other in the mud. Then he was sitting on top of me, pinning me down with his weight, and I couldn't move a muscle. He was strangling me, pressing my head into the sludge so it ran into my mouth and I could feel a death rattle in my throat. I could not let it end like this, in the mud near Zonnebeke.

GODALEVA! I must have yelled her name, as something startled the German and at that moment, in that heaven-sent split second, I felt something hard strike my arm. A bayonet! After that, everything happened in an instant. My hand gripped the steel and thrust it into the German's throat. Blood streamed through his beard and on my face as he was still sitting on me, slumped forward like a drunk on the front steps of a pub. I pushed him off me. The veterans were watching from a distance. Once I had calmed down, I crept back to him and closed his eyes.

The tree was enormous. The roots emerging from the soil looked like grappling bodies. We couldn't make out the branches in the dark. The object, whatever it was, was on the west side, about five side branches up. I whispered to Sergeant Alois that I'd climb the tree. He nodded in the direction of the hilltop, indicating he would keep watch. It was deceptively quiet, though we knew from experience that within seconds, the silence could turn into the roar of German artillery, whose scouts, ever vigilant, would fire off signal flares at the smallest provocation. I clambered up the tree. On the fifth large branch, I stopped to catch my breath. I couldn't see Sergeant Alois anymore. In the faint moonlight, I slid along the branch. The object was nowhere to be found. I decided to crawl another couple of metres further. The branch was thicker than my waist, and I wasn't afraid it would creak. I peered into the distance for a moment. Not a flicker of light on the hilltop. All was quiet. Just a little further.

At that moment, I saw it. To the side above my head, just out of reach. Darker than the black night sky. I had to scramble to my feet. My hands groped for two sturdy branches. I pulled myself upright and planted my feet wide apart. My left hand reached out. The steel surprised me. I carefully traced a finger along it. A gun. I pulled it free from the branches. It was then I heard the whistling. A flare exploded above the tree. A German keeping watch must have spotted us, must have caught a hint of movement or sound. I flattened myself against the branch, melted into it. But the bomb came anyway. A couple of dozen metres away from the tree. I heard Sergeant Alois scream. Shrapnel hit the underside of my branch. The wood shuddered under my cheek. Another one. Closer. Too close. I was blasted out of the tree, fell down several metres, curled around a branch like a chick tumbling from its nest prematurely and hung on for a couple of seconds before falling to the ground. I smacked down on the churned-up earth a few metres from the trunk, the weapon next to me, its barrel buried in the soil. Stunned, I lay still. Then I heard its wail and rush: a third bomb went over the tree. Wide of the mark. I pulled the gun out of the ground and crept toward Sergeant Alois. He was lying on his belly, pressing his hand on the stump of his arm. He could still walk. The fourth bomb shattered the tree behind us, and in a hail of wood chips and bark, we stumbled back to our troop. It was the end of veteran Alois. A shard of metal had sliced through his abdomen. I only saw it when he was lying on his back in the trench. He died in the presence of his comrades. An unheroic death. They all agreed on that. He deserved better.

Bullets missed me. Bombs exploded around me, killing others. I refused to view it as the intervention of a supreme being. Or had Godaleva lit a candle for me in her bedroom? I liked to think so.

The weapon that had nestled itself in the branches of the lonely tree was a light machine pistol of German make. The fact that it had ended up in the tree didn't puzzle me in the least. On our marches through the Westhoek, we had often seen objects hanging in the branches of trees. Once even the chest of a horse, neck and front legs dangling from it, and on another occasion part of a Hindu, his red coat flapping in the wind undamaged. But the fact that I was now holding the very same machine pistol in my hands that the late Sergeant Alois had spotted, did strike me as miraculous. This place was crawling with soldiers, each of whom would have given their eyeteeth for such a gun.

I ordered a supply of ammunition and a manual through the corporal—this was the weapon that was meant for me. It felt right.

MY TURN TO keep watch. I lay on the edge of the trench like a footslogger, peering into no man's land. It was a bleak night, the moon obscured by clouds. The cannons and machine guns were silent. I was glad of the silence. The dew was already settling on the ruined world around me. My eyelids slid shut. I dropped back into the trench, leaned against the wall of packed earth and let my chin fall to my chest. I had no idea how long I had been sitting there when a punch in my belly made me double up, gasping for breath. Realizing I had nodded off, I instinctively curled up and groped around for my machine pistol, which I was certain I had planted upright in the mud beside me but seemed to have vanished without trace. About five metres away, dark silhouettes were wrestling with each other, panting, groaning, stabbing. My fingers felt for the knife in my trouser pocket. The silhouettes rolled toward me. I distinguished two figures. No, three. One of them fell over, his head only a few metres away from me. Hands raised to heaven, gurgling. A bayonet lodged in his open mouth. Then a scream from the wrestling, monstrous shape in front of me. One man on top of the other, the legs of the wretch at the bottom kicking wildly. Which of them was the enemy? I clutched my knife in my fist. The sound of cracking bone. Head sagging. Legs convulsing. Then, all went silent again. The silhouette stood up, looked down at me. My heart pounded craters into my chest. He came toward me, panting and supple, like a prowling predator. I tensed my muscles, ready to stab him. But then he stopped, the moonlight suddenly gliding over his face, and whispered my name. And again. He bent over and picked up my machine pistol. I was still clutching the knife, even when he gave me his hand and pulled me to my feet. Only standing straight in front of him did I recognize him: Victor. A dark trickle of blood, smeared out like the tail of a comma below his eye. He had saved my life. By killing the Germans, who'd been out to get me, and by not raising the alarm, which would have earned me a bullet for breach of duty. Then, before I could say a word, he said goodbye, turned and disappeared in the maze of trenches.

TIME WAS A deranged creature, stunned by death and violence, bereft of any sense of humanity.

'They're dying for a dump again,' the new corporal said to no one in particular, eyeing the gang of veterans behind me. I sprang to attention. A young man, he had come to replace the previous one, of whom we had only found shreds of his boot. A shell had landed bang on the roof of his dugout. I had left the group of veterans to read Godaleva's letters again. In recent days, I'd regularly felt an overpowering desire to see her. Her last letter was dated a month earlier. I wondered why she had stopped writing.

Nature had presented the new corporal with an unusually shaped skull: his forehead continued the incline of the nose while his prominent lips and teeth accentuated the depth of his eye-sockets. The hunch on his back forced his neck forward. Out of the corner of my eye, I saw a movement in the troop: the famous black notebook, which also included my name—not crossed off or scratched out as yet—and in which the men casually gambled with life and death, was going from hand to hand.

'Ten days,' I heard someone say.

'If I had a mug like that, I'd teach my buttocks to clap,' the same voice went on.

'Fifteen,' someone else said.

'You'd not find a gas-mask to fit it,' a third one said.

'He got the hunch from too much wanking.' Their roars of laughter had the desired effect. The corporal handed me the pile of furlough-passes for the whole troop, his eyes darting nervously to and fro between me and the veterans, my body a shield against the banter. I felt sorry for the man.

'You distribute them, Schoolmaster. That's what they call you, isn't it?' he added with a grin, casually spitting a gob of phlegm into the snow at his feet. He pretended not to mind the comments on his appearance. But in his eyes, which looked dull and lifeless, I could see the scar. I saluted. The veterans didn't give me time to distribute the passes in an orderly fashion, they jostled around me like pushy schoolboys fishing for their report cards, and snatched the passes from my hands. They called out to the new corporal that he should take care not to shit his pants when they would be gone that night, or the muck might freeze to his bum.

In the frosty cold of early evening, we waited for the truck that would take us to Poperinge. The engine coughed to life. I was the last to leap on the platform.

'The girls are expecting us tonight!'

The veterans were as frisky as young dogs. They ordered the driver to step on it, because they all had hand grenades in their underpants. The driver called back that there was black ice on the road and that they'd end up in a ditch if he went any faster. Cursing, they hit the benches with their palms. Then one of them said to me, 'Schoolmaster! You'll be able to give the barrel of your other gun a good hard blow-through tonight!'

During the drive, I noticed that large portions of our route were shielded from view by tarpaulin that was tied to the canes in the hop fields. A giant curtain, behind which the set of the military stage was constantly changing.

We were stopped by the British. Then the French. And finally even the Belgian army itself. They checked our papers. It was dark by the time we leapt from the loading platform on Poperinge market square. They dragged me through a confusion of lanes and streets, and finally pushed me down some slippery steps and through a half open door into a bar.

We hadn't been inside for ten minutes—I had only just found a seat at the bar—when I heard a roar, and beer splashed into my face. Cheered on by their comrades, two of the veterans came to blows with three Frenchmen. They were separated and, after trading shouts, curses and threats for a few minutes, went back to their drinks. I dried my face, and handed the warm towel back to the woman behind the bar. She looked washed out. You could have cradled a baby in the flab of her double chin.

After a few pints, I started to feel sluggish. I decided to get some fresh air, wormed my way through the crowd, to the door, up the steps, into the street. A horse snorted. A group of civilians walking on the far pavement eyed a cluster of boisterous soldiers with suspicion. I walked away from the noise and lit a cigarette. I smoked it quietly, flicked away the butt that arched through the air like a flare and landed in the snow with a hiss. Two girls minced past haughtily, arms linked. Handbags dangling from their shoulders. They laughed, throwing back their heads, and chattered arrogantly, as if they already saw themselves at the centre of attention. In the distance, a chimney was spitting sparks. I turned round and ambled back to the entrance of the bar. About ten metres away from it, a lone figure stood on the pavement, legs planted wide and arms crossed on his chest.

'Evening, Schoolmaster.'

'Evening, Victor.'

He grinned. He had changed, even seemed to have an aura of calm and serenity about him. Gone was the highly strung Victor I had known, always on his guard, always lying in wait outside the Pumphouse pub.

'Thank you, Victor,' I said humbly, as I hadn't yet had the opportunity to thank him for what had happened on the night I'd nodded off. He waved my words away with his left hand and crossed his arms again.

I felt a sudden impulse to talk with him about Marcus, about the guilt I dragged with me like a foot trap. Perhaps capturing it in words would alleviate it. Victor didn't judge. Besides, the war had made any question of individual guilt irrelevant. We were all guilty. He broached the subject himself.

'There was a lot of talk about you in and around Elverdinge, just before the war. It was in all the papers.'

I confirmed it with a mumble.

'And once the war's over, are you going back inside?'

I didn't answer, trying to shape Marcus's name with my mouth, to give it voice.

'For what it's worth,' he said, 'that Sunday you took Marcus to the pond for the first time, I was there too, poaching on the estate.' He grinned at the memory. 'I know you heard me. I saw you look over your shoulder.'

'I only wanted to teach him to swim,' I said.

'I went to Ypres,' he went on, 'to tell them what I'd seen.' It touched me to think he'd gone to all that trouble for me, but I could tell from the tone of his voice that his visit had been fruitless.

'They would reinvestigate. That's all they'd say,' he said.

He gave me a friendly slap on the shoulder.

'Just make sure you survive the war, first,' he said.

'You, too.'

I couldn't imagine a German getting the better of him.

Only a cowardly bomb would be able to finish him off. We chatted for a while longer. Two sober men talking quietly in a Poperinge street that was crowded with army equipment and gangs of raucous soldiers. We were fighting in a war in which human lives were worth less than the lice in our armpits, but neither of us felt beset by death. Then we fell silent. He could see in my eyes that I had one more question.

'Verschoppen is in Reningelst.'

He paused, looked at me with squinted eyes.

'The British have put up their barracks on his farm.'

A sense of dread came over me. He wasn't telling me everything. She hadn't sent a letter for a long time, while I kept writing to her.

'Godaleva?' I asked with a pinched voice.

He didn't want to tell me, turned his face away.

'What's happened to her, Victor?'

'Godaleva; she'll be fine. She's always been more than capable of looking after herself, believe me.'

So she was alive. All the same, I felt as if the blood pulsing through my veins had turned to tar. My heart was pounding in my temples. I lost patience.

'Dammit, Victor, what happened! Tell me!'

I wanted to grab him, force the words out of his mouth with all my strength.

'She joined the nuns, to help in the sickbay. In Loker. It was hit by a shell a couple of weeks ago. She survived, though, and returned home. She's a tough 'un.'

The door of the bar swung open and the veterans toppled out. Two of them tripped over the steps and scrambled to their feet in confusion when they realized they were lying in the slush. They spotted me.

'Come on, Schoolmaster, we're going to the girls!'

They pulled me on, leaned on me, narrowly missed my

shoes as they spat and vomited. I waved to Victor. He shouted something after me, but it was drowned out by the drunken roars of the men surrounding me. I did see him shake his head before turning away. In front of the brothel, the military police were on guard in an army jeep. Seeing us coming from a long way off, they got out of the car, their hands on their holsters. The veterans noticed them too, but made no effort to temper their drunken blathering. They laughed and jabbered with everyone they met. I sensed trouble ahead and went up to one of the policemen.

'No drunks allowed.'

This was serious. Five brawny men in uniform. Armed to their teeth.

'Drunks are too unpredictable,' the one in front said. His neck was thicker than the barrel of a cannon.

The veterans were clustered behind me.

'Where's my girl?! Want to give 'er a good screwing!'

'Plough her furrow!'

'Hey, pull my finger!'

'Lie between her titties!'

'Pull my damn finger, you bloody idiot!'

'Lick her fanny!'

I signalled sharply to them to knock it off, and to my surprise, they did.

'They can be as horny as a bunch of crippled monks, they're not getting in.' The man in front again, the one with the barrel-neck. The men were getting impatient. They had quietened down, had stopped cracking jokes. I knew that at the slightest sign from me, all hell would break loose. But I also knew that in their inebriated state, they were no match for these giants. I turned and lied to the men, saying I knew a place in Elverdinge where we could go for a good time later. Without a grumble, they tramped back to the bar.

By two o'clock in the morning, they had drowned my lie in booze and were too plastered to think of girls anymore. The truck that was to take us back was waiting on the pavement. They leaned on me as I helped them all get onto the platform before leaping on myself and knocking at the cabin window. The engine started.

My conversation with Victor had left me extremely agitated, as if an ant colony were gnawing on my veins. I wanted to see her, hold her, smell her. In a moment of madness, I leapt off the truck at the Elverdinge junction. The veterans, who were lying on the floorboards semiconscious, didn't notice. Nor did the driver. I followed the red rear lights until they disappeared from view.

Elverdinge was full of French and British troops. The streets were patrolled regularly, and there were army trucks with provisions and ammunition everywhere. I wanted to go unnoticed as much as possible and avoided crowded places by climbing over the occasional wall or hedge, and sneaking through back gardens—realizing full well that in war time, a shadow stealing through the night was fair game, even for civilians with shotguns. If there was no other way—if the garden was too small or there was too much light coming from the lamps and candles—I walked through the bannered streets in the manner that would arouse the least amount of suspicion: like a drunken soldier.

The moon glowed brightly that night. Turning into Bollemeers Lane, a place I knew so well, I saw that a bomb had torn an enormous hole into the right side of the church roof. It was starkly outlined in the moonlight. Shells and grenades had gouged deep holes into the graveyard. I went in. Coffins lay on the ground in splintered fragments, one even sticking straight up out of the mud. Many of the concrete vaults, built for eternity by wealthy citizens of

Elverdinge, had also been bombed to pieces. I stepped on a sharp piece of bent metal which sprang up from my foot and gashed my shin. Cursing, I walked away from the church to look for Marcus's grave. I found it, under the tree that Godaleva had mentioned during one of her visits. The fact that the grave had been dug in unconsecrated ground had one advantage: it was undamaged.

I kneeled down before the grave. I had never spoken to the dead before, even though I'd seen so many of them. But the whites of Marcus's eyes were not staring at me now. His body did not lie lifeless in the sludge. He was safely underground, in his coffin. I was talking to something I couldn't see.

I heard a distant drone. An illumination shell exploded. Seconds later, a shell whizzed through the roof of the nave. The walls shook. I took to my heels, dove into the closest vault, where both my hands sank into a reeking cadaver, scrambled over it, crouched into a corner and waited. The German bombing of the church almost left me senseless.

I don't know how long I sat there, but by the time the noise in my head had finally subsided and I dared creep out of the stinking cave, it was morning. My eyes were caked shut with dust. The powder smoke singed my throat and lungs. What little there was left of the church was ablaze. In the distance, I could hear the engines of trucks. Human voices, calling one another. I blindly groped my way forward.

Then I heard the shout. It seemed to come from under the ground. Following the sound, I realized I had reached the front of the church, where the sacristy was. Another muffled shout. I remembered the exact location of the sacristy door from seeing it during my walks. Behind a hazel shrub, which had to be incredibly tough, as it was still there. The ground was strewn with rubble. Some of the ceiling beams had been split in two and hung in mid-air. Another shout. Crawling over the rubble, I found the stairs in a far corner. The door had gone. I called out. An answer came. Dragging chunks of stone out of my way, I descended further. Daylight didn't penetrate here. I groped my way down. The echoing voice sounded horribly close. The walls were damp. Suddenly, my foot bumped into flesh. I bent down to feel the human lump at my feet.

'My saving angel, my saving angel, God be praised ... ' the man kept repeating. He was stuck. I felt his leg, the piece of rubble, and when I had a good grip on it, told him I would try to shift it at the count of three.

'My saving angel. God be praised ... '

'I'm a flesh-and-blood human being,' I panted as I lifted the stone. He moved his leg and I put it down again carefully, helped him to his feet. My arm and shoulder supported his limping body on the steps. I knew who he was. I could have left him there, trusting his God to save him.

'Thank you so much! God is merciful! I went to the crypt to guard the Hosts, and lo and behold, He heard me! He sent a saviour!'

'I've told you before, Father, I'm not a saving angel. I'm a foot soldier of the 9th Infantry Regiment, number 775290, Private David Verbocht.'

He stood rooted to the ground on the penultimate step, as fresh sunlight started to filter inside. I pushed him forward. We both crawled out of the entrance to the crypt and sat down on a piece of bombed masonry. He said nothing as he pulled open his shirt. I noticed a thick, white belt around his belly, with some kind of metal container attached to it.

'The Hosts,' he said, tapping the metal with his finger.

'Saved by a heathen,' I said.

The church was surrounded by British soldiers with water tanks and fire-hoses.

I didn't want to waste any more time. Before I had even turned round, he blessed me, and thanked me for saving his hosts. I hurried past the Pumphouse pub, which despite the early hour was already packed with soldiers. Their drunken singing was unsettling the horses that were standing on the other side of the road, their heads in oat bags. They stamped the ground and laid back their ears each time someone walked past behind them. A column of army trucks loaded with heavy artillery approached from Vlamertinge. I realized the new corporal would by now have noticed my absence at the roll call, and that the military police would already have launched a search for Verbocht the deserter. But the thought vanished when I walked past the estate gates. On this very spot, I had seen Verschoppen disappear into the night with Marcus's corpse. A Belgian officer riding a tall stallion stopped me, saying I looked like a dust bag in boots and asking why I wasn't with my company. Without missing a beat, I invented an urgent message I had to deliver to the officer on duty on Verschoppen's farm. If it really was that urgent, why hadn't I come on the back of a galloping horse? Intelligent officers were few and far between, but one of them was in front of me now, and a malicious grin was spreading over his face. I spun a tale about my beloved horse, my trusty companion from the beginning of the war, whose belly had been ripped open by a stray piece of shrapnel. Just as I was passing Elverdinge church. And that, out of deep respect for my lost friend, I was making the rest of my journey on foot.

The officer, a horse-lover, nodded. The story didn't convince him in the least, but he left me alone and spurred on his horse.

A quarter of an hour later, I was at the drive, the ornate number 4 still blinking on the letterbox. The farm was a hive of activity, army trucks came and went. No angry barking. Perhaps Buck had accompanied Verschoppen. In the fields I saw the British tents. Soldiers were sitting on tables and chairs in the middle of the courtyard, basking in the early morning sun. No one paid any attention to me. I reached the front door and tugged the bell-pull.

Someone fumbled clumsily at the lock. Perhaps she had injured her hand, lost some fingers to a white-hot shard of metal. If only that was all it was. A heavy sigh came from the other side of the door as the teeth of the key bit into the lock with a click. Slowly, the door swung open. I jumped at seeing the figure inside. The crooked frame. The grey hair—it was Mette. With her little girl's voice and even the ghost of a smile—the look on my face probably amused her—she asked me in. I walked past her, gripped by a fearful sense of foreboding. My hands trembled as she shut the door.

Godaleva was not here anymore. He had taken her to be looked after at his quarters in Loker. After a long silence, I asked if she'd let me see Marcus's room.

The bed was made, and on it lay his long trousers, his shirt above them. Perfectly ironed, waiting for the body it would never again cover, fingers that would never again button it up. The bag on the bedside table, closed. And all around me, covering the walls, the ceiling, the doors of the wardrobe, his drawings of animals. Butterflies and birds I had never seen before, which must have sprung from his imagination. And there, at the exact centre of the wall opposite the window, bathed in morning sunlight, his last drawing: a sparkling pond, the red-brick bridge, white water-lilies, dragonflies, and on the water's edge, hand in hand, two people. A boy and a man.

I turned to go. Down the stairs, through the long hall, over the flagstones of the courtyard, between the rows of willows lining the drive. Past the ornamental number 4 on the rusty letterbox. I stopped at the spot where I'd seen Marcus for the first time, standing on the last row of cobbles before the drive met the lane that wound its way indifferently through the landscape into the distance.

Two mounted officers stopped in front of me. One of them tall and proud. He was about to dismount when the other tugged at his sleeve. Officer Verschoppen and the judge. The judge called out something to Verschoppen I didn't catch. The horses snorted restlessly, their lips flecked with foam. Their hooves clattered over the cobbles when the men left me standing there and galloped up the drive. I walked on.

The road looked deserted, there were holes where the houses had been. I stopped at Mr Vantomme's house. The roof was missing, the right-hand wall had collapsed. I wondered whether he was still inside. It didn't seem possible that he could have fled, with that hernia of his. Unless they took him away in a dog-drawn cart. My house was still standing, but the front door was gone and the window panes lay shattered on the ground. All the furniture had been burnt as fuel, I could tell by the bits of blackened metal lying around. I went into the garden. The board was still there, leaning against the wall, damp and covered in lichen. But no sign of Spiney. I consoled myself with the thought that he had probably found a safer place for hibernating.

I sat down on the ground and stared at the sky, where the clouds looked like white shreds of cotton wool carelessly plucked out of a bag. I thought of the explanation I'd once given Marcus. My metaphor for life. About the runner. The constantly elusive finish line. But it had never been that way. I had always been running alone. So had Marcus. And the finish line never budged. A short distance before it, we ran together. My legs cramped as I lay down to stare at whatever was hidden behind the clouds, behind the blue.

AN ORDER RINGS out. The men shoulder their rifles. The officer is standing in front of them, holding his sabre. He walks backward, out of the line of fire. Slowly, he raises his sabre. He's not looking at me anymore, but concentrating on the next order he will have to give. He waits. A strip of icy frost slips from a branch and falls to pieces in my lap. The veterans are watching. The winter sun behind them. I bow my head and close my eyes. I think about the beauty and serenity of the animals that showed themselves to me. Of Father and Mother, our family, the way it used to be. Of Marcus. Godaleva. Myrtha.

Of Ratface.

On the Design

As book design forms an integral part of the reading experience, we would like to acknowledge the work of those who went into creating the form in which the story is housed.

Tessa van der Waals (Netherlands) is responsible for the cover design, cover typography and art direction of all World Editions books. She works in the internationally renowned tradition of Dutch Design. Her bright and powerful visual aesthetic maintains a harmony between image and typography and captures the unique atmosphere of each book. She works closely with internationally celebrated photographers, artists and letter designers. Her work has frequently been awarded prizes for Best Dutch Book Design.

The picture on the cover is taken from the Westhoek Image Archives. It shows four-year-old Remi Berloo in 1915 in his best clothes, wearing the cap of a French soldier. The picture was taken in Cayeux-sur-Mer, a seaside resort just south of Somme Bay, where children were trans-ported to for safety during the First World War. The children were housed in an institution led by nuns and had no contact with their family until the war was over.

The cover has been edited by lithographer Bert van der Horst of BFC Graphics (Netherlands).

Suzan Beijer (Netherlands) is responsible for the typography and careful interior book design of all World Editions titles.

The text on the inside covers and the press quotes are set in Circular, designed by Laurenz Brunner (Switzerland) and published by Swiss type foundry Lineto.

All World Editions books are set in the typeface Dolly, specifically designed for book typography. Dolly creates a warm page image perfect for an enjoyable reading experience. This typeface is designed by Underware, a European collective formed by Bas Jacobs (Nether-lands), Akiem Helmling (Germany), and Sami Kortemäki (Finland). Underware are also the creators of the World Editions logo, which meets the design requirement that 'a strong shape can always be drawn with a toe in the sand.'